To: Ladd & Shirley

Enjoy all the adventure
life has to offer. And many
Thanks,

Montana
Kid
Hammer
6/09

# The Old West Adventures of Ornery and Slim

## The Partnership

*A story by Montana Kid Hammer*

authorHOUSE®

*AuthorHouse™*
*1663 Liberty Drive, Suite 200*
*Bloomington, IN 47403*
*www.authorhouse.com*
*Phone: 1-800-839-8640*

*First published by AuthorHouse 2/23/2009*

*ISBN: 978-1-4389-1997-3 (sc)*
*ISBN: 978-1-4389-1998-0 (hc)*

*Library of Congress Control Number: 2009901793*

*Printed in the United States of America*
*Bloomington, Indiana*

*This book is printed on acid-free paper.*

# Contents

# ACKNOWLEDGEMENT

I would like to acknowledge all the cowmen, vaqueros, from Spain, Mexico, and through out all of the Americas, and Hawaii, whose way of life has become my great inspiration and means by which I pen the stories that comprise this old west novel.

I am especially pleasured to my truly loyal friend and trail companion, Teddy "Blue" Abbott, who has endured many long hours; on the trail and in the woods, hearing my recounting the many numerous tales that have become so much of the material of this tome. Also, for his fair and honorable courage to constructively critique my written labors so as to aid me in producing pure prairie printed paper fictional. Likewise, I wish to recognize both Don Reed and Lisa Van Sickle from whose powerful personalities so handily contributed to the crafting of two of this storybook's wonderful characters, (Capt. Reed and Miss Lisa Brennan).

I must share my unbridled gratitude to three favorite sisters, my daughters; *Mary, Mykaela,* and *Mallory*, for their; hours, days, and weeks of verbal exchange, one-on-one editing sessions, and so much more in assisting my efforts in making this book a reality. Also, to my so many wonderful 'pards' of the Single Action Shooting Society, (SASS) who so oft encouraged me to see this book from my mind's eye to the spine bound anthology that you now hold.

Finally, I acknowledge my parents for taking me on world travels, where I gained a grave appreciation for our amazing America. Also, for their encouragement to follow my desire to share a storytelling passion via written word. And, a very special thanks to my dearest, *Aunt Joyce*, whose discourse of book writing upon me during my childhood actually inspired me to explore the possibilities of writing what I know best. Enjoy!

Dedicated to Aunt Joyce, the person, who when I was eight-years-old, inspired me to write.

Also, to Uncle Stewart, who possesses an insatiable love of reading.

And finally, to
*'Montana Sioux Beth'*

# WELL SPRINGS TOWN MAP LEGEND
## (A town formerly known as Isbee)

1. Town Marshal's home
2. a. and b. Empty lots
3. Cemetery
4. Church
5. Parsonage
6. School & schoolyard
7. Schoolmarm's Bungalow
9. Town Marshal's Office/Jail
10. County and Town Courthouse
11. County Sheriff's Office/Jail
12. Ellington's Town Bank
13. High Roller Boarding/ Card House
14. Aces High Gambling House
15. Grande Palace Saloon & Hotel
16. Imperial Bathhouse and Laundry
17. Connelly's Saddlery and Boot Shop
18. Black Pete's Smithery
19. Empty lot
20. Empty lot
21. Empty lot
22. Empty lot
23. Railroad right of way
24. Future Train Depot
25. Empty lot
26. Fletcher's Livery

27. Corral, Fletcher's Livery
28. Shipley Stage Office
29. Telegraph Office
30. Postal Office
31. Baxter's Barber and Dentistry
32. Hop-Phat's China Laundry
34. McCray Home
35. Daily Home
36. Baxter Home
37. Mercer Home
38. Bannan House
39. Ellington Home
40. The Tower Restaurant/Tower Hotel
41. The Well Spring's Daily Chronicle
42. Bonney's Bakery
43. Townsend Mercantile
44. The Europa Card House
45. Keen's Butcher Shop
46. McCray's Apothecary
47. Vandelhorn's General Store
48. Empty lot
49. Grimm's Gun Emporium
50. Lady's' Day Dress Boutique
51. Dr. Bannon's Office
52. Mercer's Mortuary

# The Town of Well Springs

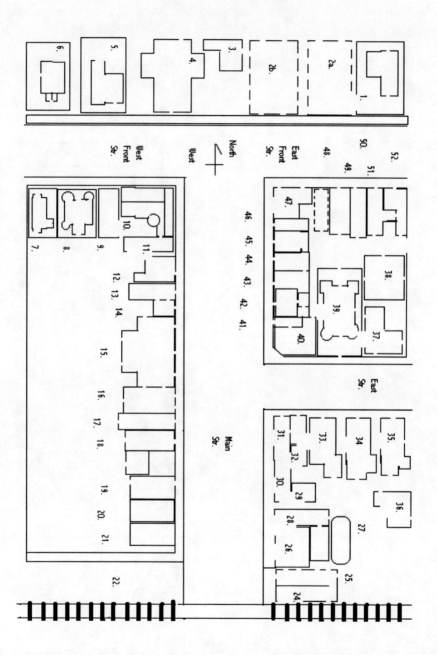

# Well Springs Ranching Community

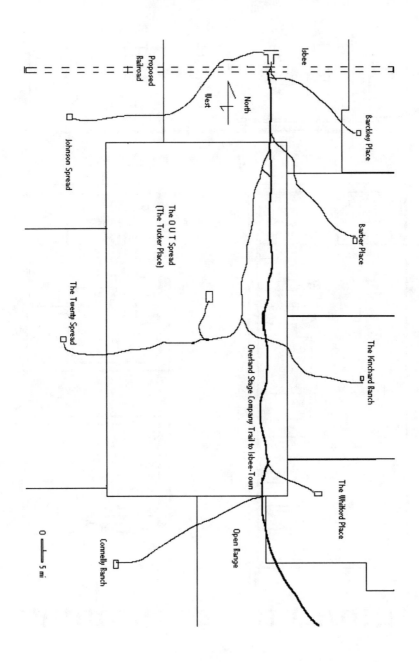

# O U T SPREAD MAP LEGEND

1. N<u>o</u>. 1 Line Shack

2. N<u>o</u>. 2 Line Shack

3. N<u>o</u>. 3 Line Shack

4. N<u>o</u>. 4 Line Shack

5. N<u>o</u>. 5 Line Shack

6. N<u>o</u>. 6 Line Shack

7. N<u>o</u>. 7 Line Shack

8. Bull Head Butte

9. Rancho, the Tucker Place

10. South Rim Ridge

11. Splendid Valley Overhang

12. Split Arch Waterfalls and Pool

13. Sorry Dog Creek

14. The Little Missouri River

15. Big Wind Canyon

# O U T SPREAD MAP

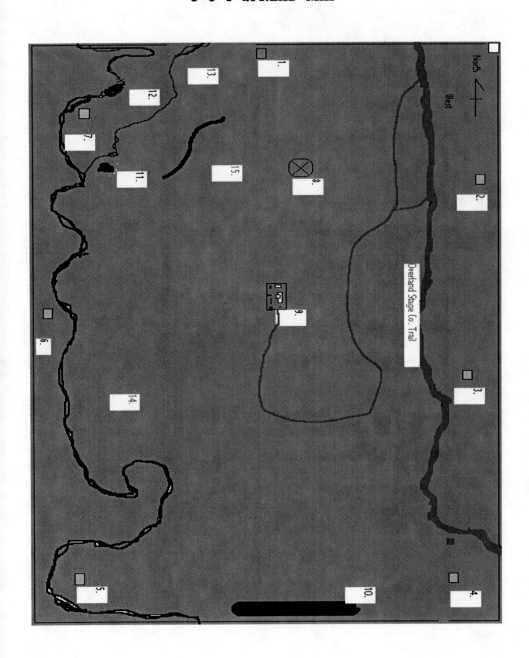

# Chapter I

## SWEET ON SLIM

Just before Slim's train left the station in Philadelphia, as he walked the aisle of the car he had just boarded, he accidentally stumbled over his own feet and tumbled unexpectedly into the lap of an incredibly startled young lady. He whispered, "Whoa" as his nose filled with the fragrance of her heavenly scented perfume. Dazed, he looked up from her lap into to her face, eyeing a stupendously demure, prim and proper look-some lass, with strawberry-blonde hair and deep green eyes. She was fully clad in a spendy lace and tonie plaid laden dress. He recognized by her attire that she was a local gal. Slim couldn't let this awkward, yet fortuitous moment pass, and spake as he swiftly regained his feet, "Oh, please do ferguv me my momentary clumsiness, Miss!"

"You are forgiven," she replied, "just beware of your feet, good fellow."

"If'n I may be so bold ma'am," asked Slim, "what brings ya' to this car today?" Cautiously glancing left, then right, she said in a low tone, shyly, "I am going west to a place called Well Springs, in the Wyoming Territory to be with my papa." Slim couldn't believe his ears and with honest wide-eyed astonishment queried, "Did ya' say Well Springs, Ma'am?"

"Yes sir, Well Springs was what I said."

"How er ya' addressed, Ma'am?" Suspiciously glancing around again, she searched to see if'n she wasn't being singled out for trouble, and then replied in low tone, "I am Mistress Denise Morgan Ellington." Smiling, he said, "That's a powerful purdy name yer christened with, and a very handsome dress yer wearin', too.

As they talked Slim learned that she was the only child, of Mr. Ethan Allen and Morgan Louise [Thomas] Ellington, of Boston, Massachusetts. Her pa was the bank owner in the cow town where Slim was going to live and work. They were headed on the same journey, in the same timeframe and Slim ruminated that this joint journey just might have the fortuitous outcome he was hoping for. So in this very first encounter the young couple's destination proved to be their very first of many striking commonalities of a partnership.

She sat back down on her hardwood seat, hard like a solid wood church pew. Slim, not wanting to be brazen, yet felt a sense of duty to his new lady companion said, "Miss Ellington, might I offer my services of company and protection to ya' since we're gonna be friends in Well Springs, and such?" With a polite smile and a wink she replied, "For this far off frontier journey of ours, I accept your offer." She felt he might need her companionship as much as she might well need his protection, and said as much to him. Slim reckoned he'd have no fuss with this arrangement, or so he hoped. He fetched his meager belongings from the seat just behind hers. All while the lady stayed quite near her bag and her reticule, snuggly.

As their train departed, going to Chicago, Omaha, and in Omaha aboard the Union Pacific railway they'd travel through Cheyenne to Fort Laramie, Wyoming Territory. At Fort Laramie they'd take hold of a stagecoach to go a trip cross-country to a little berg neither had been before, this Well Springs.

Smiling, he sat across from her and said, "I'm Slim, ma'am and I'm goin' west to work as a cowman at a place called the O U T Spread, southwest o' Well Springs, and ya'?" She replied, "Please call me 'Denise,' Slim. Besides being my pa's house mistress, I hope to work as a nurse and sing in a local church choir, if they have a church and that church a choir?"

As they traveled Miss Denise shyly explained how her papa and mama had gone west to cattle country a whole year earlier to expand the Ellington family business holdings. She remained in Boston to finish her nurse schooling. She went on to share her deep sadness upon

3

the untimely death of her mama, from small pox, upon their arrival in Well Springs, the previous autumn. After her mama's death, her papa demanded she remain in Boston to finish school and administer the settling of her mama's affairs both in Boston and her mama's hometown of Philadelphia. Only upon the conclusion of that business was she to travel to her papa, out west.

Miss Denise had gone to Philadelphia after graduation to visit her mama's oldest sister, Aunt Suzanne, who was, Mrs. Suzanne Thomas-Pritchard. It was from her aunt's home she found herself on the train that very day talking with Slim. Now he was quite sure and certain their meeting was genuinely fortuitous.

Slim told Miss Denise it was the Thomas and Pritchard families who'd procured for him his new employment out west in Well Springs. Through his half-uncle Jimmy, a Thomas, from Slim's mama's family side, was how he was related. In such manner Slim and Miss Denise were in a word, cousins, twice removed. Slim concluded that a family connection provided a second commonality in their purposed parallel partnership.

The couple's simple talk dwindled down as the lady rested herself and he gazed out the window soon growing weary with the passing scenery. After a time he pitched an appeal to Miss Denise and the passengers of their train car, one of entertaining them with simple music that he himself would play. Receiving joint consent from her

4

and the passengers, Slim produced a harmonica from his long coat and began blowing up some familiar tunes.

Before long every soul in the long car was delightfully engaged in song, while the car's wheels provided the beat from the rails, and the car's innards spilled over with melodious merriment. There was a sight to behold; Miss Ellington led the songs, Mr. Slimmery made the music, and all of the passengers, young and old alike, sang along.

Later that afternoon the train's conductor discovered Miss Denise was seated in the incorrect rail car. He stated, "Lady-Miss, you may desire to go up forward to the next car so you might receive the services your fair has purchased." Fresh off the memories of their recent camaraderie of song, she asked, "Sir, may I remain with friends, please?"

"Ma'am," said the conductor, "there's no refund on your luxury car ticket if you choose to remain here." Then to Slim's disbelief, yet pleasure, Miss Denise purchased a second Pullman car fair for her new companion, so they'd both take meals in the dining and resting cars to fresh up whenever they pleasured. They bid the conductor, *adios*, remaining at their original benches for the most of the day, much to the gratefulness of the travelers about them.

Throughout the evening of the first day Slim continued to play his mouth harp and harmonica, interchangeably, while Miss Denise and others whistled, hummed and sang along. When they slowed down to further repose, the two young folk gaily conversed so's to become

5

acquainted one to another, further. Slim and others told on yarns, fable stories, and more so's to pass the time away on their long and tedious rail ride.

"Boy howdy," thought Slim, "but that 'purdy' Miss sure could sing." No wonder she was searching for a church choir so as the angels above might accompany her. So whether this activity was his and her way of entertaining themselves so's to pass the time pleasantly was of course anyone's supposition. The fact was the folks in the railcar were having a cracker jack of a time while these two youngsters from Philly musically entertained the full car.

Following Miss Denise to the dining car for supper and back, Slim procured a set of blankets and feather pillows from the car porter for the evening. Not surprising it got some drafty in the passenger car, and later, a mite cool. The blankets proved to be an act of wisdom and mercy on Slim's part.

By ten-thirty that evening it was plenty dark outside and not much lighter in the train car as the car lamps were lit, yet trimmed to guv off very low light. The window shades in the car were drawn and Slim quietly lulled folks to sleep with soothing tunes played blown up on his harmonica.

Miss Denise politely thanked Slim for a joyous day and for the abundance of especially fine music. Slim assured her the pleasure had been his. Now it was Miss Denise who pointed out their kindred love of music was, perhaps, another commonality, too. Slim honestly could not nor would he contradict her obvious observation.

As night bore down, Slim found he wasn't sleepy on count of the earlier excitement and more. Miss Denise, though resting, showed signs of being chilled. Slim generously surrendered his blanket to her and hoped he'd not regret that decision later. Soon after, his lady friend slept peacefully to the mild sway of railcar like a gentle rocking chair. Slim fetched up his long coat from beneath his bench, covered himself and sat watching Miss Denise sleep.

While she slept, Slim faced her from the opposing bench and gazed upon her serene angelic countenance. Slim's thoughts reeled back to the earlier wonderment that'd transpired between them. He ruminated on how gracious she'd been in furnishing him with that finery-coach pass. He pondered why she'd stay in the standard passenger car when she could have easily moved to a finer ride in the luxury car.

Slim now accepted the truth of the matter that this young woman of wealth and high social posting was a privileged soul, was a finer woman than most for remaining in his and the company of many 'social less-ers', so Slim classified them. He marveled at the uncommon kindness she exhibited, much like a nurse, for which she said she was. He definitely was pleasured with the prospect of her being one of his new friends in this soon coming new home. At last he guv up his gaze and finally settled down to some much needed shut-eye.

Early the next morning Miss Denise woke in her seat looking over at her new pal, she thought, 'pard', that's how Slim would speak it, right? She was some surprised and a bit embarrassed to find that she'd both blankets and pillows, while Slim lay sleeping, having none but his road coat, 'duster' he called it, wrapped around himself and his head on his mashed hat. Miss Denise woke Slim, asking, "Would you be as kind as to escort me to breakfast, please?" Groggy-headed, Slim replied, "I'm a very willin' accomplice to this kind o' doin's."

At breakfast Miss Denise expressed her heart-felt gratitude for Slim's gentlemanly conduct toward her, the previous day and night. Yet, she sensed Slim not only shared his only blanket with her, but also watched over her most of the night to boot. She was more than pleasured to make restitution with hot breakfast for her newfound gentleman friend. And with every mile of track put behind them each one found the other just a bit more indebted to the other.

Upon Miss Denise's continuously polite insistence, Slim reluctantly told her parts his life story, for she so loved stories and knowing about her friends, especially new friends. He countered, sharing how sorely he felt his life was in no way a match for her own, yet was plenty pleasured by the way she took to every one of Slim's tales. And, this was the way the next few days transpired for the coach car confined couple.

Night after night Slim watched over Miss Denise with great care and attention as they journeyed. Eve after eve, as she slept, he took stock in how picturesque her simply elegant countenance was. Miss Ellington stood just a hair more than five feet tall. She was a petite and lean figurine, yet her slight features were strikingly bold against her exquisitely fashionably tailored dresses. She made a man's eyes as pleasured with her presents as his taste buds would have taken to sweet Swiss chocolates or fine French wines, so's Slim figured. Now guv the circumstances, her general disposition had proven to be as complimentary to life as her physical attractiveness, as he supposed.

Once more Slim supposed Miss Denise was guv to every occasion to be or, could have been; uppity, pretentious, and haughty for all of her society upbringing and more. After all, she had the finest surroundings life could offer young women of her time in this America. She'd been afforded the best; homes, life, schools, elegancies, society connections, back in Boston and Philly, and more finery than time, a pen, and paper, might scripturally embrace.

As for her being wrapped around her own axle hub, self-indulged, well, Slim didn't recognize any such gibberish residing in her radiant personage. Miss Denise was delightfully matured for her years, not twenty for another four years. Her sensibility followed that she was, now, without her mama, like Slim, and was to serve a dual roll at her papa's side as dutiful daughter, the new home's able-capable maid and community nurse. Slim guessed she'd wear all those hats superbly; he was sure and certain of that.

Alas, Slim hoped he wasn't coming down with a case of 'calico fever'*. Miss Denise wore much finer attire than calico, but he might be 'gittin' feelin' fer her'. Somehow he figured it was too late for that, if he was reading his heart properly. It wouldn't bare any likelihood they'd ever have any kind of future together, guv to their differential social stations, her papa, and all. Or…?

With nary a worthy distraction to utter of just prior to reaching Chicago, the trip was more about necessity at this point, the necessity of getting there. Lacking much else to boast about and badly bored, Slim had to coax Miss Denise very little to some activity of frivolity and gaiety upon the same car and some new passengers too. And, they did just that, entertain. Smiles and laughter come to the occupants of the coach car brought on by the stream of music, song, and stories by, Miss Ellington and Mr. Slimmery. This was how the time was slain during that long leg of their journey.

With a brief but hot and humid layover in the windy city by the lake, Chicago, Miss Denise and Slim boarded a different train, later that afternoon, going to; Omaha-Ogallala- Cheyenne-Ft. Laramie, WT and all points in between. It was there on the platform that Slim took stock of a dark character and his small band of 'nefariously* ne'er-do-wells' boarding the train, same as them. Miss Denise took stock in them as well, and suggested that Slim now join her in the convenience Pullman cars for their travels to Omaha, and beyond.

Slim was sorely pleasured to take her advice and accompany her there, but admittedly was unnerved to be in, "the world o' elegance". He was better adept at wrangling with wily desperados than doing dining dormitory dealings. All of this "fork and finery" was just more than he'd reckoned for. However, he'd learn it if she'd be enough polite to learn him how. She was a gracious travel companion and did her top hand best to facilitate Slim in taking pleasure in this exceedingly rare experience. To settle her guest Miss Denise desired that Slim tell her more about this cow craft of his. Slim obliged to share only what he did know and that he was about to receive a whole new learning, forthwith. So they chatted, chuckled, and made good humor to muse to what this new cow town way of life might be, having never done it before.

Omaha was on them to their satisfaction in short order. The trip had been pleasurable and upon a short respite, the train resumed its way west to Ogallala, Nebraska. By now the trip was beginning to wear hard on them and for reasons not made quite clear to none the train stopped in Ogallala by afternoon's end. No one was terribly disappointed when the train temporarily halted its westerly journey. The delay was a welcomed diversion from; the heat of late May, the rocking of the railcars, the sedimentary life, and the dust and cinder ash showers provided by the steam locomotive.

Slim peeled a sharp eye for that band of trouble-doers as he departed the train with his duster, warbag* and long lever gun. He made a clear display of being on the lookout for 'ne'er-do-wellers,' yet none played to open. Slim accompanied Miss Denise to her hotel where he delivered her safely. He set off for the telegraph office, a bathhouse, and a place to bunk down for the night, probably the livery stable, for he knew them places well.

Before Slim departed, Miss Denise politely asked, "Could... no, forgive me please. Would you be my special company for dinner, err... supper, if you wish?" Slim offered, "Ya' drive a hard bargain, ma'am, but supper at seven it is, here in the Main Hotel's eatery." She smiled and nodded and followed her baggage porter upstairs to her room.

It was four-thirty, post meridian, on the wall clock at the hotel desk. Slim tipped his hat and bade her, "Good afternoon, fair lady!" She replied, "And to you, good sir." Miss Denise was extremely pleasured to be departed from the train so's to repose on a real bed, in her second floor hotel suite, a bed that didn't jostle about on rails. And, once rested for a time she yearned for the occasion to stroll the main street with a book in front of her face like she so oft' did in civilized Boston.

As she walked along the street reading her primer in the evening light, a gentle early summer breeze was a consolation unto her soul as she strolled along gleaning from the printed word.  Near an hour passed by as she sat, strolled, and read her copy of *Jane Eyre*.  It never crossed her genteel judgment that this might not have been a fitting berg for doing her favorite of pastimes, alone.

Intrigued by a peculiar display of a beautiful, book reading, boardwalk strolling young dame, who was oblivious to the world around her, as a certain personage took to tailing after her.  This tall and slender fellow casually sauntered on down the opposite side of the street eyeing her with some particular interest.  He kept a respectful distance from her and held a loosely paper-wrapped object tucked under his right arm.  He brooded to himself why this seemingly big city gal, as she did appear to be, might go so carefree in of all places, a frontier town.  Upon his divided attention, this lady did disappear from him unknowingly.

Some minutes later, and all the sudden, Miss Denise's situation changed drastically, as she happened by an open space between the wooden buildings, on the boardwalk near the end of Broad Street, a party of men quickly and quietly manhandled her off the walkway.  Regrettably their business with her was, at best, one sided, ill-mannered, discourteous, not to mention outright nefarious.  Her lady virtues were now guv to chance and not to purpose.

On that summer's eve the streets were reasonably tranquil and foot traffic sparse, on the count of suppertime.  This quad-some o' ne'er-do-wells rudely harassed Miss Denise, calling for her reticule, her small draw-string handbag, and demanding a visit to her hotel room for the balance of her remaining valuables, and a little more.  Dropping her primer, she quoted for them, from the Gospel; Proverbs 1:19,

*"Such is the end of all whom go after ill-gotten gain; it takes away the lives of those whom get it!"* Miss Denise declared abruptly.

Hastily working her handbag she produced a small Colt Model 1849, thirty-one-caliber pocket revolver, in her own defense.  Initially, the men unhandled her.  But when they failed to guv Miss Denise a path out and foolishly came to lay hand upon her again, she reacted.  Her back against the wall of a local merchant's shop, just inside the portico, and guvin' her no relief from their pursuit, she swiftly shot in the chest the first man taking to tugging at her togs*.  One of the men tore from her hand her revolver and now she was sadly doomed, yet she silently prayed herself for release.

As the remaining three outlaws perpetrated their imprudence upon her, their shooters drawn and pressed upon her, they slapped her face with their 'irons' and pulled at her outer garments.  Without warning a gunshot rang out from the opposite side of the street.  A second desperado fell away from the fray.  Rifle in hand, Slim raced across the street to Miss Denise, who fought ferociously to defend her possessions and her virtue.

Slim reaching her in the nick of time and used the butt stock of his brass-framed Improved Henry rifle to whack the last two ruffians to the dirt. The ring-leader, the boss man in black, played for his belly gun and Slim used his lever gun at close range to shoot the man, the bullet catching his gun going right hand, that bullet going clean through the hand, along with the wood of the brass frame grip.

Soon a crowd of nearby townsfolk swiftly assembled round about and spoke in defense of the Ellington-Slimmery duo and their combined gunplay, in their own defense, most assuredly. Fortuitously for all parties of the fracas, they did survive the shooting, the beating, and the being pawed over aplenty.

Shortly the local law appeared and gathered up that meager assembly of unsavory, but battered scoundrels and led them away to the local hoosegow. Guv the circumstances, the lead deputy made allowance for Miss Denise and Slim to remain in possession of their shooters, but reminded them, "…they'd have to appear before Judge Jenkins's court at eight o'clock the next morn, or at least before they departed on the train, the day next." Miss Denise was covered in the blood from the ne'er-do-wellers, the black powder smudged stains and an odor of sulfur from the very close range gunplay.

"Sir," said Miss Denise, "I sincerely beg your forgiven and request of you a bit more time to clean and refresh myself before supper, please.

"More certainly," replied Slim, "take yer time, I'd have it no other way." He handed her back her leather bond book. She held it in one hand, along with her purse strings, and took hold of Slim's hand. The two walked back to the hotel. As they strolled along quietly she thought there must be something to this Slim, for he was always there when needed the most and he was goodhearted about too.

When they reached the hotel lobby she said, "Please wait for me here and I'll be back." She squeezed his hand and gracefully ascended the staircase to her room. Smiling, Slim said, "I'll be counting the moments 'til yer return." She smiled at him as she went.

Later, at the table with her companion, the same man who once again affected her latest rescue kept their supper appointment, though fashionably late. Neither was worse for the wear and her chief concern, as a nurse, was for a minor wound that Slim had suffered upon his left hand during their street scuffle. Slim was genuinely heart-struck for the level of care, attention, and concern she bestowed upon him, while owning little serious regard for her own earlier safety. Again she was beholding to Slim for his devoted personal protection of her person. He was pleasured, as usual, to be of service and nothing more, or was it 'nothing' more and would time tell?

On the morning next, once they'd been served justice, a judgment by the good Judge Jenkins, they were back on the Union Pacific train, now repaired and headed for Cheyenne/Fort Laramie. Both were highly pleasured to be alive and finished up with that band of no goods. They were equally as pleased to be going on to their new fortunes. He'd greeted her that morning as she came down the staircase and rushed to embrace him, ever grateful that he was still there.

In the railcar Miss Denise, later and once more, closed her eyes to fetch further rest, while Slim kept a very dutiful eye on her like before. As she slept, all propped up in the corner formed by the padded leather bench seat and the car's cushioned sidewall, Slim sat across from her and gazed on her enchanting face, once more.

Slim thought that perhaps Miss Denise was the most intriguing and delightfully, sweet young calico in all of the whole west; at least as he saw it. His evidence was she and her actions bore these accusations into reality. She was friendly, good-hearted, pleasant-natured, caring, and so very lovely to situate his eyes upon. Again, he marveled at her short and sweet, petite-ly slight features, strikingly bold against another of her exquisitely feminine outfits.

No doubt Miss Denise pleasured a fellow's eye, just as sweet molasses sugar candy pleasured the tongue. Her personage was the equivalent of her corporeal loveliness and she was truly a unique, a one-of-a-kind sort. She was rare enough and tricky to describe in few words. However, this young lady was unmistakably recognizable upon a lightest evenhanded description.

Slim had encountered the truth, that, she could play shrewdly in business. She was forthright, honest, and an indisputable firebrand, not afraid to utilize God or gun, when put to the test. When Slim came out of his mental fog of contemplation, out of his daydream, he thought he ought not burn holes in her by staring her to death. That certainly wasn't gentlemanly good conduct, most surely.

As pleasured as they'd been to depart Ogallala, they were sorely elated to reach Cheyenne and later, Fort Laramie, where'd they take passage on the stagecoach headed to their final destination, home. So's they stood, hand-in-hand on the train platform outside the fort, a gentleman in a dark brown suit and matching derby approached and asked, "Are you newly-weds seeking passage via stagecoach to Well Springs and points beyond?" Smiling, they looked at each other, then back at the man and in an un-rehearsed voice jointly, "Yes, please sir!"

"Follow me," he said to Slim and Miss Denise, and the four folks on the platform to their right. It was all the young man and woman could do to keep from busting out in to uproarious laughter, following the man's 'newly-wed' comment.

Within thirty minutes Miss Denise and Slim were sitting nestled tightly inside a stage, their gear stowed in the boot of that coach, and going up the trail through Wyoming. The coach ride was a hot one, plenty of miserable dust and noise, so's to trifle a soul a mite thin. Slim asked, "Miss Ellington, 'er ya' thinkin' what I'm thinkin'?"

"As a matter of fact I am, sir." So together, to their personal satisfaction they brought civility to the road. Miss Denise quietly smiled her smile of appreciation at Slim for his musical merriment in less than comfortable surroundings. As she quietly illustrated her approval, it didn't escape Slim's watchful eye. But she didn't make it difficult for the showing either. As all six occupants jostled about in such cramped spaces they labored to bring some civility to their travels.

The stage stopped a few times that day to refresh passengers, teamsters, and horse teams, before arriving late in the evening at a way station for the night. Once there, they fetched supper and slept out under the stars. This was a very new experience for Miss Denise, but certainly not her last time.

In the midst of the dark night and before anyone noticed, Slim swiftly scooped Miss Denise up off the ground, blanket and all, and rushed her to the carriage before she was fully awake. The wind, the dirt filled air was so thick and Slim struggled to get his own breath.

"Slim… Slim, what's happening?" asked Miss Denise. Slim replied, "A prairie storm, and we gotta git goin', quick up." The coach was hastily assembled and it raced to the trail, weaving, bobbing, and tipping at times, the driver and shotgun rider fighting to stay atop their ride. The prairie grit poured in through the coach from all directions, every face shielded in cloth wraps most of the day went by unseen. Later, the horrific winds brought driving rains and the dust turned to mud. The trail turned sloppy and bad slickery. The stage now had to travel much slower so's not to wreck over on itself.

As the carriage yawed and skid to and fro, Miss Denise wrapped herself around Slim's waist with a near death grip. Slim was shaken goodly for all of the commotion and found it difficult to keep his wind from her constant arm wrapped pressure. Yet, he shared to her, as he was surely thinking what she was thinking too, were they gonna die out in the west before they'd a chance to live in it… and they were so close to being at their new home. No one had mentioned to either other of this kind of peril. However, they were learning it by living it, straight up.

Slim bravely wedged himself in to the back corner of the carriage, pressured by her weight so's to brace themselves and frantically went silently along. It was there he discovered they were each softly mouthing the Lord's Prayer, of Matthew 6, of the Good Book. Looking into each others eyes, they quietly smiles at each other for this. Then she said, "You're sorely brave, Slim." He answered, "Yer truly beautiful, Denise."

By very late that evening the storm guv up, a whole other day past, the stagecoach finally rolled in Well Springs, W.T., which was a crackerjack feeling for all. Darkness filled the night, except for the few lamps lit about Main Street. Miss Denise, and finally Slim, disembark their carriage finally, both working to lose their 'sea-legs' from all so many the days of that ride. Mr. Ellington, a man of medium height, a stately build, and brownish-gray hair, bright eyes, and handsomely attired, was there to make claim of his daughter and her belongings. Slim was guv a hand scrawled note with his instructions from the town telegrapher who manned the stage and telegraph office.

Later that night as Slim lay on the bed in the hotel room, he pondered back on his journey westward. His thoughts of Denise dominated his ponderings as he smiled to himself. Miss Denise seemed so very content to be home with her pa and for having had a grand adventure with her new in-training cowman friend. Slim thought of her boldly placed request of him before they departed company that night, her papa at her side, "that he should come for supper upon the very first opportunity he received." Of course, he'd be blissful pleasured; 'clean up past his saddle cinch' for her company, providing her papa guv his approval. Deep down Slim figured she'd have her way with her pa's thinking.

In the hotel that night Slim lay deliberating his fortuitous travels as he gently drifted off into a deep sleep. As his thoughts faded away he figured riding the range for Mr. Tucker wasn't gonna be all that tough if there was a beautiful and charming mistress, that was, well, sweet on Slim. And all things guv, would Slim buck up as a fitting cowman on this O U T Spread and would time, deed and spirit tell on Slim?

# Chapter II

## AN ARROW SHIRT AND A CUP OF COFFEE

Whoosh! An arrow flew past and stuck in the trunk of the tree right next to Ornery. He rapidly filled his right hand with his trusty old Colt '73 Cavalry revolver and rose to his feet in the flash of an eyelash. With the lightning slip of his thumb and trigger finger he shot with deadly precision at the swiftly approaching camp encroachers like in the day when he was a mounted trooper. Slim swept the brass-framed Winchester "Yellow Boy" lever rifle from his lap and stood up as quickly as his partner. Slim barely heard the tin cup in his lap, or felt the warm coffee splash as the cup tumbled down to the ground when he stood and to put that rifle to his shooting shoulder.

Slim anchored his feet in place but felt something ever so lightly tug his right shoulder back a bit, and hard. Ornery yelled, "How many o' 'em do ya' see out there, lad?"

"Three, four...no FIVE!" hollered Slim, as almost everything disappeared into a thick blue-gray sea of gun smoke from their pair of trusty shooters.

It took a moment for Slim to figure out his situation; the shouting, shooting and his blouse being unexpectedly taut about his neck and right shoulder. For now his attention was heavily centered on the rifle's front sight and the swiftly approaching horse riders.

"Ornery, are we kil't now?"

"No, they've only got us surrounded, so's weez got 'em now. Keep shootin' up a storm or ya' just might be!" So's the two did just that, shoot up a storm.

With the abrupt attack on their campsite Slim recognized he didn't own the luxury of a momentary distraction to figure out why his collar was so unbearably tight, and all so suddenly. Whatever hampered his ability to operate the rifle smoothly made him discover he was able to hold and aim it like never before in all his born days. And with that newly found ability he shot down the attackers, one by one, as they barely appeared to his front sight.

In mere moments four bodies lay dead near Slim and when nothing loomed before him he ceased his rifle fire. Yet he held steady just in case he needed to shoot again. After what seemed like an hour, yet just a long minute, he lowered his rifle from his shoulder so's to figure why his collar was still gnawing at his neck so.

All the while Ornery shot his handgun dry and rapidly fished into his bottom vest pockets for more .45 Colt caliber cartridges. In a flash he punched out each spent case from each cylinder hole, via the ejector rod on his revolver, and dropped a fresh cartridge in its place. His revolver reloaded, Ornery shifted his stance letting his left foot lead and raised his long barrel to point shoot the fast moving encroacher. As he blazed away a warrior's lance whizzed past his hatless head cutting his left ear and slicing his scalp open. Ornery felt warm blood trickling down behind his ear, neck and soak into his blouse.

Ornery hollered, "Ow!" He flinched backward hard enough to throw himself off his feet and falling on his back in the dirt. As he fell, Ornery hung up his right spur on the log seat behind his boot where he'd been sitting moments earlier. He emptied his handgun on another figure rushing him, straight on, knife in hand. The attacker was so close and came with such speed that the body fell dead, nigh on top of him. Everything faded into a thick cloud of gray gun smoke around Ornery.

In a flash there was no more whooping noises, shooting or shouting. This was slowly replaced by the sweeter smell of the Ponderosa pine, the cool of the light breeze and the sound of gunfire echoing though, horse's hooves beating a path out of the sparsely spread stand of trees where Ornery and Slim made there fight.

24

Slim turned his head to the left away from his rifle sights and toward Ornery who didn't appear unblemished.

"Ya' gonna stare me ta death, or 'er ya' gonna come and fetch me back onto my boots?" shouted an upset and a suddenly embarrassed Ornery.

As Slim lowered his lever gun he found himself stuck solid in place. From his peripheral vision and to his right he spotted his solid problem. An arrow was stuck to the tree just behind his right shoulder, at his back. It missed Slim's flesh but penetrated his oversized right shirtsleeve at the shoulder before tacking itself and his blouse snugly to the tree trunk. This now explained why his collar was drawn so tightly about his neck and why his rifle had held firmly in place as he hung tight in his blouse during the shoot out.

Ornery watched on in curiosity as his bunkie attempted to pull himself free from the tree and said, "Ya' gonna git off that..." Just then, Slim's navy blue woolen blouse tore loose from the tree where it had been held firmly. Slim pulled away from the arrow like he did and when it ripped loose he awkwardly became unbalanced and wrecked himself to the ground in a dash. It was no laughing matter, but Ornery couldn't help himself as he finished up saying, "...tree?"

Now Ornery wasn't born with the name, 'Ornery,' but rather, Patrick Jason O'Connor, an appropriate name for an Irishman from southern Kentucky. A renowned horseman and schoolteacher before the war, (Between-the-States, circa 1861-1865), he serviced as an enlisted Confederate cavalryman. Twice Slim's age and a few more, he was a tall stout brawny square-jawed sort, silver-haired that once may have been some reddish, blue-gray eyes and twice Slim's girth, and a powerfully strong man both in build and will, well built for a saddle. He got branded, 'Ornery', by his outfit because he never cared for taking senseless orders or a sassing and at times could be just plum ornery! This Slim would come to know as the truth and in short order too.

Slim hurriedly scrambled back to his feet and gathered his bearing while wandering his way over to Ornery who was lying on the ground. Slim grounding his rifle so's to free his hands and aid the injured cowman. Dazed by his fall, Slim's eyes were still blurry-some and he'd a fit getting a focus on his ground-bound partner.

"Ya' ailin' any?" Slim asked. Ornery shook his head, no, but pondered a double moment while he assessed his own situation and guv thought that perhaps Slim ought to be asking himself that very same question. Instead, Ornery answered, "I don't feel no holes in me anywhere, or no busted bones, I think?"

Slim stood there a long moment looking down at his pard with a big smile and said, "Ya' gonna marry that carcass Ornery or 'er ya' gonna crawl out from underneath it?"

"Go ahead, laugh!" replied Ornery, "Ya' think it's grand to be funnin' my misfortune, don'cha, lad?"

"I do and I will and I'm gonna laugh me some good one on yer account," answered Slim. "Yer wearin' that carcass like some kinda blanket and it just looks queer some to me from where I'm a standing'!"

"Would 'cha just help me git back to my feet?" Ornery shouted.

"PLEASE!" said Slim, a smile on his face. "Ya' gotta say please, Ornery?" And of course, the only "please" Slim got was a harsh scowl from Ornery. Slim came over and dragged the dead man's carcass off Ornery. He returned and offered his right hand toward his ailing pard and aided Ornery back to his feet.

"Ya' sure 'er true to yer nickname, Ornery!" Slim said, as he grasped the older man's right hand and pulled him back on to his boots. And Ornery's "thank you" to Slim was a second grumpy groan and ornery glance.

Once back on his feet Ornery realized his right ankle was twisted bum from his earlier stumblings. Slim hastily fetched Ornery a log seat to sit him upon next to the campfire. He pulled off his very own 'kerchief and fixed it around Ornery's head to cover the lightly bleeding head wound, the one caused by the narrowly missed lance. Slim looked about the camp while cinching down the bandana bandage. Fortunately, their two horses had weathered the attack, both alive and tied up to their tether rope. Everything else looked no worse for the wear so Slim reckoned knowing they was a fortunate set to still have the horses and their hides guv just what'd happened.

As he sat himself down at the fire pit he pondered the attack on the camp and a question came to him and he asked, "Where'd 'em encroachers come from like that?" Ornery shook his head implying he wasn't sure, for certain, as he looked over at the younger man. After a moment Ornery piped up, "I'm figurin' that they's some renegade-ed up Cheyenne's and I'z guessin' that they was a lookin' to 'whack us down havin' off with our critters* fer their very own, like buffaloes." Slim nodded in agreement, as he figured that was a fair a reason as any.

Suddenly, and without warning Ornery let go a good old belly laugh as he nigh on rocked him off his log seat-resting place. He pointed to Slim and the big wet spot all over the front crotch of Slim's trousers. He laughed his words aloud, "Em Injuns scared ya' good an' hard, huh Slim? Look what'cha did ta yourself, pard'! Look down, yer' all wet…"

"ORNERY!" Slim interrupted his bunkie, yelling, "Ya' bite yer tongue, ya' mean ol' cuss, fer I ne'er did no such a thin'. This all happened when I stood up and my tin cup spilled my coffee all down my front!" retorted Slim. After Ornery stopped his laughter and recomposed himself a bit, he turned to Slim.

"Crackerjack story there, pard!" Ornery said. "Boy howdy, that's the way I'd tell it if'n I was ya'!" Slim just shook his head not offering another word. He saw no need to get windy in his own vindication on count of that old coot. Ornery had a nose and knew the difference between coffees, and well, 'wet'. Slim didn't fail to notice how Ornery took great pleasure in funning him for being knitted to that tree by an arrow earlier, and now this wetting himself. However, Slim did have to agree that his wet trousers did look a bit suspicious, even though he'd almost disremembered the coffee spilling on him when all the hoorah commenced earlier.

In the end, all's well that ended well. Slim, with the aid of his trusty long gun and Ornery, they saved themselves and their small herd. Truth be known, and all the funning aside, each was admirably pleased to have survived as they tried their best to stay that way, in lieu of an arrow shirt and a cup of coffee. And, this was just another day on the trails of the O U T Spread for these cowmen on that day. When it wasn't bullets, arrows or boredom fixing to kill them, so's they figured, were they really ready for meeting up with the cowman neighbor boys of the XX Spread and live to tell of it?

# Chapter III

## WHO'S RUSTLING WHOSE COWS NOW?

Tall, lean, slim, and it was also said of him, "He's hard to shoot at cuz he weren't as fat as a rifle's front side blade," which is mite thin. Being a Slimmery made him plum 'slim' on two counts no less. Ornery was sorely quick witted, a durable character, and a man true to the western code. All of these qualities were gonna be a blessing on a day where men were 'whacked down for doing their own craft.

On this day the two cowmen rose from their bunks before first light. Ornery limped across the floor of the musty smelling, dim lantern lit shack going toward the short little black stove to rekindle the fire in his very harshly faded red long-handle underwear, boots and hat. Slim drowsily fumbled into his duds, all while thinking aloud.

"I'm sorely pleasured we're up here at ol' N̲o̲. 7 line shack, Ornery. For trouble, meaning folks with guns ne'er whoops up on us any none here." Ornery instantaneously busted out laughing, "Bunkie, ya' bite yer tongue about such thin's. We live on the open range here and trouble can, and will hun'cha down like a coyote to a rabbit, and any ol' time it desires to."

Ornery's words opened Slim's mind's eye and woke up his senses of seeing swift coming encroachers, flying arrows, smelling the campfire and fragrance of the Ponderosa pines, and gun smoke so thick he could taste the taste of sulfur in his head and on his tongue, which, he thought, was better tasting than the campfire coffee that day. For the moment, Slim was no worse for his thoughts, though it caused tiny beads of sweat to form on his forehand without control. In the low light he was happy Ornery never saw the beads of sweat.

Later, as the two chewed the fat that morning, as they idly partook of vittles and belly wash cooked up by Ornery guv tell to there chores for the day. Since Ornery cooked, Slim washed the soiled dishes. Sneeringly, Ornery warned, "Don't wash the belly wash pot, like ya' done did yesterday, cuz it ruint the pot's cookin' in flavor." Slim wasn't sure if that was a good or bad sneer or if washing that pot done it what he said it did so he quick-up changed the topic, "Whata we gonna do with 'em five beeves we found belongin' to the Twenty Spread?" A long silence hung in the shack.

"Nothin'!" replied Ornery, his telling tone saying he telling caught the change of topic, "not 'til we head to the home place, then we'll run 'em o'er by the Double X."

"Does that meet with yer likin's lad?" Slim didn't respond right away for rare was the day when Ornery asked him for blessing upon their plans, him a greener and all.

"Yep!" Slim answered, not certain if that was the proper answer or not. Ornery rose from his chair at the table where he'd finished scribbling in the line shack logbook about the last day's doings. Ornery reached over fetched up a badly worn and outdated picture mail order book, and headed to the cabin door.

"Why do ya' write in that book ever' day, Ornery?"

"Cuz I can, and fer it's my job to scribe in the logbook so's to guv proper ranch communication to anybody who needs to know o' it. Now I'm headed to the 'white (out) house' to read me up this here photo book." Now Slim laughed, "Ha! How's it ya' read photographs, Ornery?"

"Ya'll have to figure that out fer yerself, lad." And out the doorway he went hurriedly. Inside the quiet shack Slim hummed a snappy tune as he washed away on his dishes and jumped with quite a start.

"KA-POW! KA-POW! POW! POW! KA-POW!"

Gun fire; so loud, so close, and so sudden, the heavy cast-iron griddle leapt from his hands and into the wreck pan full of water, "KER-SPLUSH!" Slim could feel the water from the pan splash down his blouse and trouser front just as he wheeled about and rushed to the front wall of the cabin. On the wall next to his bunk was his heavily weathered and worn "Improved Henry" lever rifle. Slim, his hands dripping wet, grabbed his rifle as he approached and featured his thin form cautiously by the cracked open he made in the door. Spying suspiciously through the narrow slit he saw what was pure trouble and Ornery was in it.

Thick gun smoke, burning sulfur, Ornery lying prone and the sound of bullets pinging off the outer wall met Slim's shaken sanity. He, a greener, didn't waste rifle cartridges making smoke and calling undue attention to himself. Rapidly gauging his situation, Slim shoved his rifle barrel out the door, using the thicker wall and door for cover. Running a rapid lever and trigger, he made his rifle sing and sling lead on those, "no-count" bushwhacking rustlers, or so he figured.

Moments earlier Ornery loosed up his catalog and filled that same hand with his Colt revolver from off his hip. He dropped to the ground swiftly, nigh on parting him from his breath and hugged up the ground behind a trough, not far from the shack's front door. The commotion broke out so briskly Ornery didn't recognize the shooting saddlers that were fixing to bust down the corral and rustle out the critters belonging to the Twenty Spread. In this push Ornery didn't figure he should poke out his head to gaze at who they were just this now.

Ornery snapped off a hasty shot from his revolver, his bullet hitting and splintering the top of a corral post, the wood and lead splinters ripped into the face of one of the rustlers trying to pull down the corral. When he heard rifle fire coming from the shack at his back, he smiled, and shouting over the gunfire, "It's about time ya' started earnin' yer keep around here, BOY!"

"Quit'cher bein' so derned grateful," called Slim, "Besides, I thought ya' said it was better secure up here?"

"It was 'Why-Oh-You' that said that, not me," growled Ornery. "Just shoot and hush yer belly achin' 'bout secure!" A hat from one of the rustlers' head flew through the air and another gun filled wrist was shot through by a rapid hail of rifle fire shot from Slim's handy shooting.

A voice sang out unexpectedly in the direction of the shack and trough, "Hey, O'Connor…O'Connor…is that you o'er there?" Ornery lay on his side for a swift moment trying to figure out who he was hearing, "Who wants to know with a gun in his hand?" The answer came back, "It's me, Dutch Hammond, *segundo*\*o' the Twenty Spread." Dutch was a short stocky black-haired fellow, not much to look at, affable, yet held a commanding presents among his own cowmen.

Ornery shouted back, "Hammond, what kinda straw boss attempts to dry gulch his old friends? Don'cha know that we're yer neighborin' *rancho* line shack or was ya' aimin' to bushwhack us?" Hurting good from abruptly throwing his body on the ground, Ornery wiped sweat and dirt from his brow with his neck-bound 'kerchief. Puffing to get his wind back and following this ordeal Ornery stood and dusted himself off.

Slowly, one by one, the cowpunchers outside emerged from their points of refuge and converged about the water trough where Ornery stood. Each man was now wore a sheepish grin instead of a hand full of iron, gun, which was more to Ornery's pleasure. It seemed Dutch and his boys hadn't figured on saddlers from the O U T keeping the shack about this time. They hadn't seen the ponies belonging to Ornery and Slim. Heck, Dutch didn't even know of Slim for they'd never been made acquainted to the other.

"Dutch, ya' musta lost yer hat rack fer not 'recognisizin' yer old friend and shootin' up my place," stated Ornery.

"I'm sorry Ornery, but I came late to the fracas and didn't see the face of the man comin' from the shack," Dutch confessed. Likewise, Ornery shared he'd never shot back if he'd got a good look at who was a shooting at him first.

"Strange how thin's happen when a 'hurry' busts out," mumbled Dutch.

"I sorely reckon," Ornery replied. All the cowhands nervously snickered as they milled about the shack front gathering their hats, gloves, ropes and all that'd scattered during the shootout.

Slim sensed the danger had past and came out of the shack guardedly to meet up with Ornery and the Double X crew. Spoken shyly, Slim said, "Well, good thin' nobody got badly hurt or killed in all of the mis-thunk fun." Ornery's good pard, the Yellowstone Kid, was famous for sharing, "Cowmen wasn't ne'er any fancy by gunplay, anyways." Perhaps Kid was on to something with the testimony of the shooting that transpired day.

In short order the cowhands and beeves of the Twenty Spread were on their way home at last. Smiling, Ornery turned to Slim and said, "Sorry fer callin' ya' 'boy' and guvin' ya' guff about not shootin' earlier. Ya' done showed great sand backin' me play, lad." Slim said, "Don't concern yerself by worry, weez pards and I did my due." Ornery replied, "Capital good shootin', too, Slim." He replied, "Thank you, Ornery!"

Now both men turned about for the line shack to finish up putting it in proper order for the day. Looking to Ornery, Slim asked, "Whata weez gonna do about this here partly tore down holdin' pen?" Ornery smiled answering, "Well pard, weez need to be mendin' on it straight away fer our fences need be; always ready, horse-high, bull-strong and o' course, pig-tight, don'cha reckon that here?"

"Pig-tight!" Slim queried. "Since win was weez pig farmin' on the O U T?"

"Whoa thar, lad," Ornery replied, "don't git'cher bob-wire (barbed wire) wrapped around jer wagon axel so swiftly. I ain't ne'er done said weez e'er keepin' pigs here on the Spread. All I was meanin' was we ain't wantin' no feral nor domestic pigs comin' from else place to be gittin' inside our corrals, fences or pens. Ya' follow me? Not keepin' 'em in, but keepin' 'em out."

"Swell good," answered Slim, "ya' had me frettin' thar a moment, cuz I cain't cotton to neither the odor nor the manners o' 'em critters any none."

About this time, Ornery looked at Slim and looked at him some more, not believing his eyes, again. He started laughing at Slim saying, "Look at ya', yer all wet down the front of yerself again, and it don't look like coffee to me?" Slim just shook his head, laughing, and he ambled into the shack. He held his tongue knowing he'd never live down any of these shooting stories.

As it turned out no one was a rustling no one's cows anyhow and Ornery was quite accurate when he shared that good communication was very important, like in their logbook before a shootout commences among neighbors. A proper change of good words would've quit up that shootout before it was.

Now it wasn't even eight o'clock in the morning yet and another day of cow business was very much underway on Ornery and Slim's corner of the O U T Spread. And speaking of neighbors, Ornery and Slim would soon meet some new ones, even more different than the last ones, and just right around the corner as well. Who would they be and what would it mean for these two cowpunchers and their cow craft livelihood?

# Chapter IV

## POWERFUL TAR MEDICINE

On this morning, yet somehow different feeling as Slim sat his pony Pete and peering down from a short ridge top at a bawling calf standing on level ground. He also spied a cow heifer mired in a tar filled bog hole and her young bawling calf not far off. Slim pondered his situation carefully. Then a very heavy hand grabbed and shook his right shoulder good and guvin' Slim a thorough start. At that very moment Slim's ears caught an all too familiar voice and sensed he was in for, "*another one of those kinda days.*"

"Ya' gonna sleep this territory into statehood or what, lad?" Ornery called out.

Swiftly sitting up and wiping the sleep from his eyes, Slim immediately recognized the voice of his bunkie. He struggled back to consciousness from the deep dream world he'd been 'riding' in. It was then that he realized he was lying in his bunk at ol' No. 7 line shack, up in the hills, on that nor' west corner of the O U T Spread, in the midst of the pioneer west.

"What time's it gittin' to be?" Slim asked.

"It's time to git up and out to doin' chores," Ornery stated, "so's ya' best git to yer britches and boots, buck!"

The two cowmen fetched up breakfast, cleaned up the shack, and saddled up their ponies for a full day's ride on their corner of the spread. As they rode down the path, the one that led south from the shack, the sun shown warmly at their backs from over the top of the hill.

"Will we be home to the shack before dark, Ornery?"

"Yep, if'n all goes well and ya' do yer part we will." And them boys quit up the shack and headed out to fetch their beeves.

During the morning both saddlers rode up and down the bushy landscape searching for late born calves and stray beeves to gather on home. At mid-morning they split up and rode the adjacent ridgelines keeping sight of each other while searching draw bottoms for cows.

Spotting a hefty lone coyote and thinking it odd for this time of day, Ornery, sitting a top his mount swiftly took to, racked, and shot his much patina-ed brass framed Henry lever gun at the varmint. As his rifle report rang out, unexpectedly, Ornery's *cayuse*\* blew up trying to loose off the noise making rider from its back. Off balance in his saddle, Ornery cut lose of his rifle as he fought like an eight-legged Texas tan tarantula to hang on to his ride and the ridge edge that he and his pony were perched upon. If'n he didn't stay with his horse the two would likely tip right off the ridge and wreck in the bottom of the ravine. He could feel the ridge top getting smaller and the edges getting closer by him and his ride as he fought to stay where they was. The rifle report caught Slim off guard and he swiftly glanced in Ornery's direction hoping this wasn't another attack for he'd all of that he could tummy from the last attacks of the past few weeks.

When Slim glimpsed his partner across the way and wasn't expecting to see what he saw. Ornery's rifle flying into the air, the beast under Ornery seemingly going in six directions all at once, and Ornery's arms flailing as he tried to keep on top of that going everywhere beast. At first Slim was amused by Ornery's circumstance, but then it donned on him that he'd better get over there and lend his friend some assistance. He didn't desire to lose his bunkie to a fool-hearty accident this far from home.

Seeing a narrow land bridge to Ornery, Slim rode swiftly across it to his partner's side of the ravine. As he rode toward Ornery, he chuckled a grand chuckle as he watched his saddler partner entertaining the whole west from the back of that four-legged beast. Galloping to where the one-man rodeo was shaking, Slim arrived to see Ornery finally rein his horse to a stand still. The big man was plum tuckered out puffing for his wind and a touch cross from his wild horsy-ordeal. Slim refrained from any callous remarks for the moment for everyone's sake just this now.

The pair sat on their horses a time while Ornery caught his breath and out of the blue, Slim was the first to spot a calf, in the low brush, near the meadow floor. Had it not been for Ornery's handy work with his lever gun the young cow might have been a coyote's dinner that afternoon. For an instant Slim felt a strange tickling wiggle in his tummy for this whole scene seemed so inexplicably familiar to him, just like the dream he'd that very same morning. Still winded, Ornery called out to Slim as he pointed to the calf's mama.

"Ya' see… what I see… o'er there?" Slim turned and looked in the direction of Ornery's pointed finger and replied, "Yep, I sorely do!" He watched both the cows and Ornery as the big man fetched back his errant lever gun.

What they saw was a cow heifer in a small pit, or tar bog. In this pit was a mixture of mud and crude oil, oil that bubbled up from beneath the surface of the earth and seeped to the surface, mixed with the air to dry and harden some and formed a bog hole. When rainwater settled on top of this mixture the cow must of figured she'd found herself a watering hole. Evidently this heifer had no nose and so's she waded down into the 'water' and there she was, stuck in this mixture past any chance she had of treadling out from it. Well, the long and short of it was Ornery and Slim had to remove her from that messy hole.

Ornery figured the each of them would throw their lariat loops to latch her horns and they'd carefully ride away from the bog hole with the heifer tethered from their saddle horns to pull her free from that hole. They commenced to do just that after Slim finally hit her horns with his *lasso* loop, but not before Ornery guv him heck for being "no kinda header man with his *latigo* string."

The two men labored a fair ten minutes muscling from on horseback, with rope, at that poor heifer against her will to loose her from the bog. Suddenly, Ornery called out to Slim, "Ya' got socks on, today?" Dumbfounded by his query, Slim pondered to what that had to do with anything they were doing just this now.

"Do I look like I'm goin' to church ta ya'?" Slim replied. And now Ornery was perplexed, his face all wrinkled up like a paper bag. Slim continued, "No, I ne'er put on any socks, not lessun' I'm goin' to church with my good boots, so why ya' askin' ME that here and NOW?"

"First o' all, ya' don't need to get haughty with me, young mister!" Ornery said. "Now fer I need ya' to git down from yer horse, strip off your duds and go down in there, and help git that heifer a goin', that's why!"

"Who made ya' the boss o' me?" asked Slim. "I thought weez pards, so why do I gotta to go in that filthy hole, huh?" Surprisingly enough, Ornery held his tongue and spake in a mild manner, "Weez pards, Slim and this here cow is gonna expire soon if'n we don't start workin' like pards, and git her outta here, okay?" Getting Ornery's meaning, Slim nodded and backed up his pony until his string went slack.

Slim looked around good, hesitating, for he didn't truly want to commence to this going in that hole. Then he kicked down off his saddle and slowly started shedding his togs* down to his dull gray long-handled underwear. He hung his hat string about the horn of his saddle figuring he'd no need to mess it up playing in that foul smelling pit. Being a true tenderfoot he put his boots back on his feet until he got to the hole. Before Slim climbed in he removed his boots as he listened to Ornery tell him how he was to work with the heifer to aid in her extrication from the tar pit. As Ornery talked, a pair of riders approached them from the east. While they watched the two approaching riders, with curiosity, Slim went to putting back on his boots and later, his hat.

The two riders were Lakota-Sioux Indians, both traditionally attired. They came plodding up the trail on their pinto ponies going at Ornery and Slim. As this pair halted their ponies before the cowmen, the man in a black hat spake, "How…"

"*Hau!*" said Ornery to the pair o' men interrupting the man in the black hat. Again, the man spake, "I am called Spotted Hawk and this is Bull Elk Man, and how may we help you?" Spotted Hawk wore a black 'Boss of the Plains' hat, was articulate in English, had gray eyes, black hair, was a shorter man, and clad in a red deer hide 'war-shirt', black buckskin trouser and charcoal beaded moccasins. Bull Elk Man, a very tall, strong, silent, a black haired and blue-eyed man wearing a beige buckskin outfit and headdress.

"I'm O'Connor and this here is my partner, Slim," Ornery replied. "It's good o' ya' to ask, but we'd not have ya' gittin' soiled or hurt here workin' our cow, thanks."

Spotted Hawk nodded politely to each cowpoke, "Will you let us ask the 'Earth' to give freely your cow and then we will go away from you here?" Spotted Hawk inquired. Ornery looked at Slim, Slim looked back.

"I'm curious to what Spotted Hawk means and now I'd like to see this, okay?" Slim asked of Ornery in a low tone.

"Yes, please! Ask the earth to let the heifer go on outta her," Ornery requested, letting his lasso go slack, as he sat his saddle, curiously. Now it was the cowmen's turn to watch and learn from their native brethren upon this, their ancestral land.

Spotted Hawk and Bull Elk Man, with a deerskin pouch, dismounted their ponies and sat on the sod nearby the bog pit. Ornery and Slim looked on intently as they observed the two Indian men doing something that appeared to be part prayer and part mediation. From the contents of their medicine pouch the two Lakota men made smoke on sage with fire and ceremonially covered themselves in the smoke of sage, smudging, and sang a chant-like song that neither cow saddlers barely hear nor fathomed.

Next they sang and danced around the tar-hole in a clockwise direction. The two dancers stopped a short time at each of the quarter marks along their circle, the points representing; north, east, south and west. They appeared to be offering; song, words or prayer and tobacco, and Ornery couldn't properly say which, as he watched the pair do what they did so methodically.

The dancers repeated their ritual dance three more turns, and then returned to where they had stood originally and sat once more and finished with more song and incantations. If that wasn't how it commenced, it was the best way them saddlers knew to say of it.

"This's fascinatin' and kinda entertainin' all at once," Slim said to Ornery in a whisper, "but when's the cow comin' outta the pit?"

"Wait-n-see, okay lad?" replied Ornery. They watched and waited impatiently wanting to be about the rest of the day chasing their beeves.

In a couple of minutes Spotted Hawk and Bull Elk Man rose up and walked back to Ornery and Slim. Spotted Hawk spake with much medicine, that is power and healing in his tone, "O'Connor, gently pull your heifer, like before, but slowly." Ornery nodded and complied with Spotted Hawk's instruction. As Ornery and his horse backed away the rope gently tightened up between his saddle horn and the cow. With a mild struggle and slippery waddle the heifer came loose from the tar pit was standing up on the level ground and calm, like nothing had ever happened to her. Slim's nose told him that cow was soiled but his eyes saw she was no worse for her ordeal. All four men watched, in anticipation, as the young calf approached his mama with some curiosity for her oiled up smell. Slim walked over and loosed the lasso set off the larger lady bovine.

As Slim worked, Ornery twisted about in his saddle and fetched his fresh blanket out under the cantle of his saddle. From his pommel bags, lying beneath the saddle horn, he pulled out a drawstring bag of tobacco. Once he'd procured his items Ornery swung down from his saddle and walked toward Spotted Hawk and Bull Elk Man. Ornery, in full gratitude, offered his blanket, tobacco, and a couple silver dollar pieces to Spotted Hawk for setting his cow free. He then offered to fetch the men supper back at the line shack, but they mentioned their desire to continue on toward their encampment up north, on Powder River, a good day's ride away. With friendly parting words, the Lakota men forked their ponies and rode away as peaceably as they'd come.

Still puzzled, Slim queried, "How'd they do that and all, Ornery?" Ornery a bit bewildered himself just looked his pard dead on and said, "Slim, if'n I'd not seen it, I'd not have believed it myself. They may've took the fear outta her, or perhaps they're just blessed that way I reckon."

"How come ya' guv 'em yer blanket, yer silver and tobacco like that?"

"It's a long story that'll have to share with ya' another time," Ornery said, without batting an eye, "but, I was bein' neighborly as we need to git done up here and workin' theses beeves back to the shack, and pronto." As Ornery put one foot in the stirrup he turned to look at his partner, "So what are ya' doin' standin' around here nigh on naked in yer under duds?" he said, teasing Slim. "We done got more work to do, Mister Slimmery!" Slim just shook his head and smiled back at Ornery.

"Seein' ya' like that brin's to mind a story," Ornery said to his bunkie, as he looked down at Slim.

Ornery commenced to telling his tale, "I was ridin' down along the *Rio Grande*, down in Texas, late one hot summer afternoon, lookin' fer strays, when I spied me a *sombrero grande* just a floatin' on some mud and water. So's I got ta cogitatin' that that cover was a much larger sunshade than what adorn my head at present, and I ought to have it fer my very own. I cut down off the trail and rode out to where that big ol' sombrero lay. I dismounted my big sorrel at water's edge so's to go fetch this *largo* head cover. Takin' good care not to topple into the depths o' this muddy ol' ooze, I gingered my way across the muddy path along the river's edge until I arrived at that big hat. Upon reachin' that *sombrero*, I lay hol't to it and to my wild wonderment I discovered a Mexican fellar beneath the *sombrero*, and he was' a wearin' it no less. '*Buenas tardes, senõr*', I said, with a hint o' surprise in my voice, 'Might I guv ya' a helpin' hand, a rope or somethin'?'

'Oh no, no, not-tat-tall,' replied this Mexican fellow in a thick Spanish tone. 'Fine am I; fer a brawny burrow under me have I,'" Ornery finished telling. Both saddlers commenced to laughing a good chuckle fer that big windy. As Slim stood next to the tar bog there on the high plains in nothing but his underclothing, hat and boots, Ornery was pleasured to learn that his young bunkie could be an easygoing partner, all while being funned. They was pleasured to be done wrestling that heifer out of the hole and for the much-appreciated assistance from their Lakota neighbors.

Now it was Ornery and Slim's turn to guv up the line shack lifestyle, which they'd sorely miss, to return to headquarters, the 'big house'. Slim, still very new to live at the main ranch and thinking he knew his partner pretty darned well by now, was in for a socio-culinary adventure he never even ever saw coming.

# Chapter V

## THE O U T BOYS AND HELLFIRE IN A BOWL

As they ambled on pony-back down the trail, Slim said, "Ornery, it'll be a pleasure to be back at the out home place." Ornery stopped, twisted around in his saddle and eyed his bunkie hard and straight on, "It ain't 'out', ya' greener!" Ornery rudely proclaimed, "Don'cha knows it's pronounced, 'Oh', 'Ewe', 'Tee' and didn't the *segundo* learn that clear to ya'?"

"Well, if'n 'why-oh-ewe' will recall," retorted Slim, "I ne'er met him yet, so there!" When Ornery heard his young partner's hot words, he smiled, "Ha-ha-ha, ya' needn't git so arrogant on me li'l mister! Here, I'll s'plain ya' how we got dubbed up the 'O U T' Spread."

Ornery commenced his story. "Well, Mr. Tucker, our boss and ranch owner, came from Texas, north, ta W.T.* lookin' fer a brand to 'ply to his newly come herd. At the territorial brand office in Cheyenne, Mr. Tucker searched fer a brand suited to his likin'. A brand that wasn't

49

in use by a neighbor man's mark and one that wasn't easy to rewrite, or doctor up so's to appear like another brand markin' and cause his beeves to be rustled away stolen. With no mark discovered for his own he guessed he'd be without a brand fer his herd in his part of the territory fer the time or so.

The brand officer asked, 'Mr. Tucker is 'O', 'U', 'T' your paper mark, your signature?' Mr. Tucker affirmed it, for it stood for; 'Oliver Ulysses Tucker.' So the brand man shared, 'he oughta mark his herd, same as such, brand 'em with the, O U T.' So that's what Mr. Tucker done did and that's how we become the, O U T Spread, here on the northeastern Wyoming hills and prairies."

Slim sat his saddle a time taking the whole story in and wondering if'n Ornery was just funning him some or telling him the truth straight up. He wasn't sure, so he just nodded and kept his mouth shut so's not to get funned even more than usual by Ornery. The two cow-saddlers resumed their ride toward their *hacienda,* the big house.

It was very late and dark out when they finally arrived the home place. Both men parked their ponies at the hitching rail in front of the bunkhouse. Pulling down their blankets, saddlebags and long guns from off their riding rigs, Ornery said softly, "Slim, stow yer gear on the floor next to the first empty bunk, just inside the door. Then go to the barn and put our ponies to their stalls." Slim answered, "Sure, boss." Ornery headed on up to the main house to report to Mr. Tucker and the *segundo*, Cap'n Stuart, who were waiting on him as Slim took both ponies away to proper care.

Slim stepped inside the man door, lit the coal oil lantern, and fetched back to the horses back through the main barn door. He uncinched and pulled down each saddle, placing it on its respective rack in the tack room, his place being at the very end, while Ornery's was nigh on first. Sweat soaked and smelling like a wet dog, Slim removed both wet saddle blankets, placing them on the top a rail of an empty stall fence so's guv'em air to dry out properly.

He next led each animal, separately, to a stall, removed the headgear and hung their bridle on a peg next to its saddle. Slim fetched back a bucket of grain, and a currycomb and brush set where upon he commenced to trough feed the horses. As they fed, he caringly brushed and combed both animals' coats to a fine shine. He stowed his comb and brush in the tack room, climbed to the hayloft and tossed down fresh hay. Slim closed the tack room door, checked each stall gate latch for closure, extinguished the lamp, shut the barn door and walked to the bunkhouse to find himself some much desired shut-eye.

The ponies' care wasn't only Slim's manner taught to him by Ornery, but was the duty of ever cowman who earned his very livelihood with one. He aimed to do this well and then his own care, in that order, for it was their way, the code.

Both men finished their business and arrived to the bunkhouse at the very same time. With little ceremony the two undressed in the dark and got to their bunks for a short night's rest. Once home they were glad to still be alive after some weeks up in the hills nor' west of the home place.

Early on the morn' next, the whole the crew from the bunkhouse headed to the cook shack for chuck. They filed through the door and sat themselves down, ritualistically, at their usual chairs around their tables like clockwork.

The regular cook was off in Well Springs procuring up supplies, so Hap was doing up vittles that morning. He didn't know cooking like Mr. Samuelson, the ranch's Negro head cook, that everyone called "*Coosie*" or Cookie. Now that man could fix up vittles and it was the chief reason many a cowman remained with Mr. Tucker's brand, beside Mr. Tucker's fairness of the code.

Now Hap stewed up something like chili; with stringy ground beef, pinto beans, chunks of fat back, and chicken eggs thrown in, "fer texture", or so he said. Along with that he baked a batch of badly burnt cornmeal bread and a big pot of truly dusky, thick and harsh tasting belly wash burnt badly, as well. Ornery wasn't at all pleasured up by them vittles one bit, but held his tongue, which was truly a rare and miraculous event unto its own. He stood up and went off to the cupboard next to the cook stove and fetched out a bright white cotton bag marked by bold red '*Xs*' like this - '**XXXXX**'.

Back at the table Ornery sprinkled a light dusting of this dull reddish-brownish powder on his chili meal and stirred it up plenty swell. Slim took notice of Ornery's doings and that odd looking powder. Slim asked, "Wha'cha got there in that bag, Ornery?" Ornery replied, "It's Habanera pepper powder and it makes food taste a whole bunch better...it truly do!"

Slim, once an orphan; wasn't one to complain about the taste of his vittles. He just shoveled it in with haste and was simply grateful and pleasured for it. Also, his knowings didn't recollect any such pepper powder, as was this that Ornery said of either. How-some-ever, today, he did notice the greasy taste and feel, and the stringy course texture of the badly ground up meat. His tummy might take to it, but his taste buds were taking a purdy bad beating aplenty. The look on his face caused Ornery to motion a finger towards the bag of spice, indicating Slim should ought guv it a try. Slim took hold of the small stiff cotton bag and pulled it across the table to himself. He took his spoon and scooped just small pinch of the powder and tossed it over his chili stew. Stirring his breakfast good and thorough like he'd seen Ornery do, Slim took a big mouthful.

"Now this's a whole bunch better!" Slim declared.

"Please, take more if'n ya' desire, lad," offered Ornery, a sly smile on his face.

Slim took him up on the offer and put a quarter teaspoon of powder on his stew and stirred it up again. Ornery suggested that he get more chili out of the kettle and then spice it up properly, and that's just what Slim done did.

When Slim came back to his spot at the table with more scorched cornbread a top his bowl, he put another hefty spoonful of powder in the bowl and stirring it once more. Before he could take another taste of his meal, Ornery spake saying, "Would cha' please fetch us back a pitcher of water lad?" Slim thought a moment, and once more got up from the table, only to return with that water pitcher from the bar on the other side of the room, and he sat his seat once again. He filled Ornery's cup, then his own and set the pitcher on the table in front of himself. He commenced his eating.

Slim scooped up a big spoonful of that flavored up chili and shoveled it in and everyone sat quietly watching him. Initially it tasted quite zesty, but just as he set to shovel in that second spoonful; Slim's eyes nigh on bulged out of his head. He bolted to his feet like lightning, tiny beads of sweat formed on his forehead and his face changed to a deep dusky red hue. He grabbed his cup of water and poured it down his gullet getting nearly as much water on him as in him. He set down his cup and grabbed the pitcher, and tried drinking even more water.

Momentarily he discovered the water caused the pain to worsen more fiercely, so he decided he'd best get outside, out into the cooler morning air.  Slim started off the left side of his seat and tripped over his chair in the doings of his awkward departure.  He picked himself up off the cook shack floor in an all fired hurry and tried again to negotiate a path outside.  This time though, Slim got stumbled again by the table leg and nearly toppled the whole table over on Ornery.  Ornery and the other cowhands at the table caught and steadied it as Slim wandered back onto his feet and headed for the door like a wild mustang in a pure prairie pyre panic.

By now, all but Slim were doubled over with laughter; tears streaming down their faces, their sides aching and their wind now short from excessive laughter.  The young greener was a putting on quite the show by now and he wasn't even outside yet.

Slim raced to the shack door where he pushed and pushed with all his might so's to put it open.  Now everyone at the ranch knew the door was to be pulled, not pushed.  So finally Ornery got up and swiftly moved Slim aside from the door and pulled it wide open for him.  Ornery called, "There ya' go lad, out with ya'!"  Slim thought his head was on fire, his ears ringing, his eyes streamed tears steadily, his throat burning wildly and he'd no voice to speak of whatsoever.

As it was, Slim was a greener on the outfit but proving to have the makings of a top hand cowman.  He was a rapid learner and no one called him anything but a reliable puncher, good for his word, which was bore out well by his actions. However, from time to time, the old hands enjoyed funning the tinhorn kid as they did to all the new hands of the brand. And, well, today was no exception.

Slim bolted from the shack and right into the water trough, where upon arriving, he plum threw his whole self therein. He was busy splashing around when all of the hired hands, them O U T boys, poured out of the shack to watch more of this morning spectacle. After a good splashing, Slim stopped dead still, sat up in the water trough, and stared at his newfound audience. Upon stern, yet searing sarcasm, Ornery spouted, "Slim, it ain't no kinda good manners to depart cookie's shack without stowin' up yer bowl and sayin' a pleasant "thank-yee" before ya' leave on out." Laughter erupted again and Slim stared daggers back at Ornery for Slim wasn't able to verbalize himself for his burning throat fire.

Hap stepped out onto the porch of the shack so's to discover what all the commotion was about. There he saw Slim sitting in murky trough water, half submerged. He declared, "Ornery, I can tell this's yer doings, so guv the pup a hand gittin' outta the trough, would'cha?" Ornery did just that and helped the poor, wet, dazed and chilled Slim from his self-imposed bathtub. As Slim stepped from the trough and stood on the level Ornery noticed Slim had his pant legs tucked inside of his boots and water showed clean to the top of those boots. Ornery asked, "Slim, ain't cha glad it's not church day, fer ya'd got yer socks all watered up." Having heard enough guff, Slim took a half-hearted swing at Ornery and missed him clean.

Slim missed him clean, but his water soaked blouse sleeve slung a heavy mist of water all over the men standing to his front. Slim mouthed a soft whisper, hoarse by the pepper-powder stew, "That wasn't very kind of ya'… ya' cusser, you!" Once more the boys set off in hearty laughter at Slim's expense for the continued grand show. True, they all loved to work, but they loved to play just a little bit better. And today, well, Ornery had set the tone and Slim played through.

Hap spake up, "Slim, go on to the bathhouse and git cleaned up. Ornery, ya' go to the bunkhouse and fetch Slim a dry set o' duds to wear, please!" Ornery answered, "Maybe Miss Ellington could come and dolly ol' Slim up o'er at the bathhouse?" The bunkhouse boys let out a, 'HOORAH!' The horse wrangler, Wyatt Kilpatrick shouted, "Hey Slim, when yer done gittin' all dolled up, ya' come back and have all o' Hap's chili with that ol' powder that ya' can tummy!" They laughed one last time that morning on his account.

Slim shook his head and set off for the bathhouse. As he ambled, he too started to laugh as he could once more utter words with volume, his voice, just now beginning to recover from his spicy breakfast. A bit later that morning Ornery met Slim at the bathhouse to deliver Slim his fresh togs.

"I'm sorry that I let cha' git into so much o' that pepper-powder and I won't do that in the by-in-by, agreed?" Ornery asked sheepishly, as he extended his hands toward his young pard. Slim nodded, smiled, and reached out to shake Ornery's hand.

"I won't ne'er complain about Hap's cookin' e'er again, either. I believe I'll just stick to cornbread, beans, fat-back, and belly wash in the future!" answered Slim.

Slim finished putting on his clean togs and the two cowmen headed back to the cook shack. Slim did just what he said he'd do; cornbread, beans, beef, and lots of coffee. The two headed out for another long day of laboring with the cows, crafting their skills on the O U T Spread...and well, Slim was now a wiser lad for doing so, learning from Ornery his craft. And also for his brush with Ornery's devilishly killer hot, Habanera pepper-powder. What else were Ornery and the O U T boys going to learn him up, or would it finally do him in as that pepper powder nearly did? Yet, one ought to be careful what he asks for, or about.

# Chapter VI

## SLIM AND THE COW CRAFT

Digressing back to when Slim was a cow-puppy, brand new and the freshest cowhand of the O U T Spread. In the absence of the foreman, Cap'n Stewart, oft' called the '*segundo*', Mr. Tucker; met, welcomed, and showed Slim about the home place. Slim really pondered what the rest of his life going to be like and what would he be taught, as per the ad he'd answered all them weeks back in Philly? That question raised; his answer came in the tale of how he first got met up to his very first official day of cow crafting and Ornery, his pard. All Slim prayed for was that he was up for the challenge and that he'd live long enough to earn his first 'roll', so's to share it with Miss Denise.

Now **Hap** had come from the Spread to Well Springs for supplies and fetch back Slim to the ranch. Upon their return to the same, Slim was guv over to the ranch owner where he was taken to the cook shack to be met up with the ranch membership, the cowhands of the herd, them O U T Boys, as it were.

"Mr. Slimmery," said Mr. Tucker, "this cantankerous gentleman here is, 'Ornery' and you will fair well to be mentored by this top hand cowman, for there's none better." The boys in the shack busted out in laughter. Slim, not amused, took that their laughter meant this was not a good sign, yet Mr. Tucker was the boss and he'd abide it.

Already standing, Ornery raised his hands to hush this rowdy crowd and have them show respect to Mr. Tucker in the *segundo's* absence. Ornery stated, "Boys, don't confuse the young lad and don'cha mess with him fer he's mine, Mr. Tucker's orders, ya' follow?" Slim now pondered deeply as to what he'd gotten himself here with all this. And Mr. Tucker said, "Boys, let us be done of dinner and headed back out to the herd. Ornery, you make Slimmery welcome to his new home here on the O U T." He turned and left the shack as the boys got back to their chuck. Slim shyly joined in, seated next Ornery where he would remain for some years to come in that shack.

As they headed for the bunkhouse that morning Ornery looked his new bunkie up and down for measure and stated, "Well, Mr. Slimmery, I 'pect I oughta learnt ya' some o' the ways we do business around the O U T Spread while ya' er gittin' checked in. Will ya' go fer that laddie?" Slim nodded again bearing a gentle smile and asked, "If'n ya' don't take offense sir, please just call me, 'Slim', and not laddie or nothin' other."

"Fair enough, Slim," said Ornery. "Ya' can stop with all that formality now that weez away from Mr. Tucker and the 'big house'. Just call me 'Ornery', ever'body else does!"

"Certainly, Mr. Ornery!" said Slim, a hint of humor in his craw.

"Good one, lad… I mean, Slim," answered Ornery. Ya' got a sense o' humor I see and that'll pay ya' han'some around these parts if'n ya' hope to last out here punchin' cattle." Ornery paused a long moment, then said, "Now as I sez earlier, here's how we go 'bout business, if'n ya' hope to stay whole and keep yer longevity. First, in front o' this 'brand' and e'erbody that's got meanin' to ya', ya' be a man o' yer word. Second, in the bunkhouse and ever'where else on the Spread, carry yer load and don't let nobody do all the work." Slim wasn't certain what this 'longevity' stuff was, but knew about doing his share of work as he'd been doing that all his life, thus far.

When Ornery and Slim finished up in the bunkhouse they strolled over to the barn's horse stalls, Ornery piped up again, "Let's talk us about horseflesh and all, since we're headed that way. First, these here animal belong to the outfit and are assigned to ya' by the wrangler. That's Wyatt, about this here place. The animal is yers to borrow and care fer, and even Mister Tucker must ask of ya' permission to run yer horse or horses. Second, lessen yer ready to hun'cher hole, don't be foolish and mess with another man's horse without his express permission. Once yer saddled up and mounted, don't crowd or cut no man off lessen yer willin' to do battle with him. Bein' yer a greener around here, folk might forguv once, but don't count on it."

Next he said, "Treat 'cher horse better than yer'n and don't guv it too much work. I'll help ya' on this one 'til ya' get the feel fer the work we're doin' about the Spread. Also, don'cha ne'er jump yer animal into a hard run if'n ya' both have a long trail to travel, s'ept fer a stampede or yer under attack by ne'er-do-wellers or savages. Otherwise, fer success, be sure ya' pace yer animal fer the duration o' the trail. On the trail or on the drive, don'cha ta bein' wavin' yer hat, jacket, or nothin' when ya' are approachin' horses, cows an' other riders. If'n ya' do, all kinds o' calamity might commence to befall ya' like gittin' shot or stomped, so don't do any o' that."

Then Ornery continued, "Always choose the simplest route when climbin' up mountain trails or steep wet or muddy hills on horseback or on foot. This'll save on the pony and the rider both fer the long haul, if'n ya' know what I mean. If'n yer in the ponies' country and ya' ain't certain fer certain about how to go, guv the pony its head and likely the beast will git'cha through back home. And lastly, if'n ya' got to have words with another man and he's standin' on the level, ne'er talks down to nobody from horseback. If'n their on the ground, git down outer yer saddle, so's they don't take offense, lest yer by his place and he don't invite cha down. Ya'll live longer that way. If'n they're in the saddle, same as ya', remain there." Slim thought a moment about them words and then nodded.

As they reached the barn door Ornery opened a man gate and let Slim pass through then coming through he closed it.

"Ya' be certain that ya' close ever' gate behind yerself lest ya' are tol't, otherwise," stated Ornery, "don't e'er fergit! Ya' won't see many gates where we're goin' today, yet if'n we find any we'll be sure to close 'em. Yet, we'll be sure to close the ones we encounter over at the Barckley Place, fer sure," added Ornery.

Once in the barn they went into the tack room. This room was well kept, full of saddles, saddle blankets, bridles, combs and brushes and so much more, well kept. Ornery put off his saddlebags from his shoulder and fetched on his spurs. He went to Shorty's tack peg set and grabbed a worn pair of spurs and handing them to Slim. Ornery stated, "Don't let Mr. Tucker, Cap'n Stewart or any member o' the brand see ya' puttin' inee (any) hard rowel marks on inee o' our stock's flesh. Fer if'n ya' do ya'll likely end up with the marks o' spur rowel across the face or a Colt revolver barrel on yer head, and that's the true o' it." Slim understood perfectly well, smiled good and nodded once more.

Some more Ornery spake, "Learn this too, don't ne'er cuss another man's dog, fer it shows disrespect fer the animal and the man who owns it." Now with a shifty smile Ornery said, "How-some-ever, if'n the beast attacks ya' outright, kill it straight up. It's just that simple! Fer if'n that man cain't manage his mutt, then it's deserved on him. And speakin' o' not cussin' another man's dog… ne'er filch another man's woman, either. I hear tell yer sweet by that new an' purdy nurse from town, but I thought I'd mention this fer yer own sake fer the future." Slim nodded again and smiled back at Ornery, so's to show that he catch the message. Also wondered if news like that always traveled so rapidly out here in the territories. Slim said matter of fact-ly, "Miss Denise Ellington's her name, Ornery." Ornery replied, "Yes, yes, Miss Ellington, I'll try to reckon on that henceforth."

The two punchers took to finding their best day ponies and put to saddling them. Both built their riding rig with a rifle filled long gun saddle boot. They tied their slicker covered bedrolls up under the saddle cantle once the saddlebags were set. Ornery placed his pommel bags on the saddle pommel, situated over and beneath the saddle horn. Both men hung their *latigo* strings cinched up right of the same horn.

As they did this, Ornery, once more seized the opportunity to share with his green friend, "A clean saddle blanket is more important than clean bed sheets on yer bunk, don't cha know?" Slim just let go a good laugh for Ornery's analogy. Slim said, "I know my saddle blanket's the foundation o' a good day's ride in the saddle. I also know a sullied blanket will rub my trusted steed raw if'n that what yer gittin' too." Ornery acknowledged Slim's statement in the affirmative.

They prepared to depart the horse corral, their ponies all geared up, and Ornery said, "Ne'er make a habit o' havin' no one wait on ya', especially the *segundo,* or one o' his workin' parties. This's a show o' disrespect and insubordination most plain, and simple. Speakin' o' waitin,' we'd best git to the trail ourselves and *pronto.*"

Once Ornery and Slim were all set a top their rides, they took to going off the big yard going nor'east to meet up on, Hat Carrington, Chance Yocum, and a short herd of 200 beeves headed for to the Barckley Place, to be sold to Mr. Harry Barckley.

Riding up the trail, Ornery shared on Slim more cowhand wisdom "Always trail the gentler surfaces rather rocky hard trail faces where ya' cain to favor yer horse's hooves. Doin' this will bein' less wear on the horse's hooves and shoes, too." He continued, "When we meet up with the herd today, take yer assigned spot on the drive and end the day in the same place, between the same two riders, no matter whether ya' cross; gullies, coulees, hills, prairies or rivers. Slim nodded soberly and hoped he'd do his very best, from start to finish. Slim spied Ornery knowing smile of reassurance.

Yet somehow it nagged at Slim's heart to know or maybe just test to why all of this 'wisdom' Ornery had been jawing about was so proven, so he had to ask his mentor a proving question, "How's it ya' knows this all so well and yer alive too tell about it so good, huh?" Ornery caught the wee sassy tone in the youngster's sayings and yet admired the young lad's spirit for testing for the truth rather than being lead like 'sheeple', sheep-minded people, the dreaded nemesis of the cowman, to the slaughter of untried wisdoms and false truths. He answered, "Slim, don'cha 'pect that good judgment comes from experience, and most o' that experience followed a lot that come outta bad judgment? A time'll come win ya' git learned about some other folk that, well, got ett up by a whole buncha cowman bad judgment and ain't with the brand or this world any long. That's how I know, and you'll come by the knowings, if'n ya' fetch up sufficient enough longevity by keeping my sayin's an' such. Ya' follow me here?" Them words and Ornery's sincerity of saying them was plenty sufficient proof that he, Slim, would pay well and fetch long-life by keeping his mentor's taught wisdoms, and so he planned to put all of them into swift practice, henceforth.

Appointed by time and trail, Ornery and Slim met with Hat, Chance and the herd, and prepared to push on to the Barckley's. It was a small herd the boys moved, so Ornery took point, up front, Hat was on left flank, Slim on right flank, and Chance was saddled on drag, or cow's tail, the back end of the herd. The going was slow and steady, at a cowhand's pace, as Ornery put it, as they continued on east by north east to their rendezvous place. Slim rode handily to keep his side of the herd in line formation. He was fairly new to the saddle and especially to the way of herding beeves. Yet, for a greener he was doing well, with some assistance from both Ornery and Chance. Slim tried his best to remember all that Ornery had shared on him that day, yet his head ailed him for all the knowing so soon. Slim was surprised at how fast he was pressed into the field, but was grateful to be doing more than riding a train and a stagecoach. And, Slim thought Ornery wasn't as ornery a partner to be working for as he'd first figured.

The four cowmen moved the herd until just before flat darkness the first day. Slim was plenty ready to be done up, too. Slim had first night watch on the herd shortly after a simple prairie supper done by Ornery. As the darkness closed on the plain and the herd; Ornery joined up with Slim to learn him the proper way to ride about their small collection of bedded down cows. After a couple of circles around the herd, Ornery took his leave and returned to the small campfire.

Soon enough Slim fetched his harmonica and started blowing a gentle tune to settle both the herd and himself as he rode his watch. Later on Chance replaced Slim at watch. He told Slim, "Capital idea, ya' blowin' lullabies ta da herd like dat." Slim simply replied, "Thanks." Then he made for camp and was thrilled to go off to his easy blanket tossed bedroll. Long about first light and with a plains breakfast of fruit filled air tights, jerked beef, and fresh belly wash; they busted camp and threw their herd back on the trail.

By mid-day the O U T herd was fresh upon the pastures of the Barckley Place and to Mr. Carl Barckley. Once the sale was made good, Ornery and crew turned their ponies for home on behalf of a very long day in the saddle to reaching there. Slim was plum pleasured to be done and headed back.

At two o'clock the next no so moonlit morning the four finally reached the ranch and was pleasured to be home at long last. As the saddlers finished up their ride, Ornery turned to Slim and said, "We'll put away er ponies before we turn down er bunks."

Based on the cowmen's range etiquette Ornery touted, Slim knew his pard wasn't, 'stringin' a whizzer' for it was true, his words were. Slim was aware of what Ornery had been learning him and he got the meaning of each and everything Ornery had explained. Slim was appreciative of what Ornery taught him too. When they finished up their horse chores Ornery said, "Ya'll do good to remove yer spurs before going inside the big house." Slim replied, "I'll do just that." And that they both did.

Bedtime hadn't come soon enough for Slim or for Ornery for that matter. It'd been an eventful two days and a busy new start for Slim at the ranch that was his new home. While he'd not yet met Cap'n Stewart or most of the crew quite yet, he knew that would happen in due time. He'd have to come to know the head wrangler and the riding stock, in short order as well. Slim knew he'd soon learn the cow craft in good time as the newest member of the O U T Spread.

With the cow craft, cow thieving, range wars, and more going on about him, Slim pondered most as to just who was Ornery really, and was there any good in him and his kind? Perhaps he was about to learn more than he wanted to know.

# Chapter VII

## LEARNING MORE THAN HE WANTED TO KNOW

In the surrounding hills the summer season was fading fast as fall hauled down on the backs of Ornery and Slim swiftly. Come the morning they'd join other buckaroos so's to push their portion of the outfit's herd down out of hills and back to the home place for fall roundup. As usual both men were looking forward to coming home to have a catch up time with their calicos, providing all proceeded as planned, which was rare.

Late evening was mighty mundane until one singularly simple question chanced Slim.

"Slim, where's yer housewife?" asked Ornery

"Where I always've her. Where's yers, ya' lose yer housewife or use er up?"

"Shame on ya' or good un ya' Slim, now guv yers up so's I cain sew-cinch up my busted chap pocket flap."

"Why din'cha jus' say ya' wanted my mendin' kit an' I'd fetched to ya'."

"Well lad, that's what I dun did tol't'cha, so git ta it, pronto-case, we're burnin' daylight."

"Ornery, it already dark out."

"All the more reason too, so what it is now lad, yer housewife er what...please!" Slim fished his kit from his war bag and guv it to Ornery.

As Ornery laid down his mended chaps and readied himself for bed down that last evening, he noticed Slim milling about acting a bit queer so he asked, "Hey, what's eatin' on ya' this evenin' lad?" Slim sat on his bunk silent for a time and looked over at his bunkie. Slim shyly asked, "Who's Captain Reed, and why's it ya' yell and scream in yer sleep so much at night like ya' do?" The room fell suddenly still, so still the only sound there was that of the fire crackling in the cabin stove. It never occurred to Ornery that others ever noticed or even cared why he was that way or did what he did. Ornery figured everybody knew why and that's why they never asked, until now.

Eyeing Ornery's face Slim felt strange all the sudden; so awkward he couldn't look at his partner any longer. He cut a quick glance at the stove and back to the cabin's dirt floor. Ornery was taken aback and bungled his initial attempt at words. He thought Slim's question was a fair one, but never had anyone asked him about this before now.

He'd half dis-remembered about his war days and liked it that way, or had he?

Seeing his cohort was tired, uncomfortable and struggling to find fitting words for a courteous comeback, Slim said, "Ya' don't have to if'n ya' don't want to, cuz I don't need to know any such stuff, really!" Wearing a gentle smile Ornery said, "I reckon if'n I'm gonna keep ya' awake nights I owe ya' a story, don't I?" Slim was a loss for words here; because he un-disremembered how sometimes Ornery funned him. He wasn't sure if'n this was gonna be one of them times or not. Slim was truly curious about this Captain Reed and more, or he'd never chanced his question. However, the tone in Ornery's voice said more than Slim desired to learn.

In a strange way Slim was witnessing a side of Ornery he'd never noticed prior to this. Slim shook his head and once more said, "Really, I don't need to know." Ornery didn't want to share his past no how, but as a top hand cowman, knew he owed it to Slim to wise him up on the harsher realities of life. The elder rose from his bunk and went to cabin stove to stuff more wood inside. Again it was silent therein, except for the fire rumbling in their black short pot-bellied stove.

There was always a noise of some kind going on inside the small dwelling, yet the two had gotten so acquainted with them they never noticed, but for some reason, just then, the sounds stuck out in their ears as if these were all brand new. The boys sat speechless and soaked up the strange kind of stillness.

Dumbfounded by Slim's plain speak, Ornery pondered its meaning for something deeper. And again it'd never occurred to him that others might have noticed or care why he was and did, as he did. Slim felt so queer, so awkward; he could hardly peer upon Ornery, still. Looking at Ornery, Slim witnessed contortion and anguish a tired and numb mug, as Ornery struggling for words for a proper comeback. Ornery nodded and said, "I ought to be more forthright to ya', lad." Slim was surprised by Ornery's sudden uncharacteristic generosity.

Slim shook his head insisting, "Really, I don't need to know." Slim's eye followed Ornery as he went over to the water bucket to ladle his tin cup full of water. He offered to fetch Slim a cup of water, Slim declined. With his cup in hand Ornery returned to his bunk and sat while Slim looked on. Ornery sat there hunched over some in his heavy socks, light gray two-piece under suit and staring.

Staring Slim through, Ornery said, "It was that dern'd north-south war, and the stuff in my head that won't go away easy. That's what makes me do and say the stuff in my sleep. As for Captain Reed, well, he was the best derned-est Confederate cavalry commander I ever did know. He's right up there with ol' Cap'n Stewart I reckon." Silence reigned again in the small dwelling, and then Ornery told Slim a mighty powerful story of the man, Captain Reed and that north-south conflict. The story brought a tear to the eyes of a man that seemingly had no more tears to shed about loss and suffering, and Slim saw it all there before him.

Then Ornery told of the horrid sounds of death and dying he'd witnessed in the days when he was just a few years older than Slim was presently. Ornery shared of the time, during that war, when he was a riding peaceable through a small grove of trees with his cavalry unit. This was the first time Ornery had heard the odd sound of the queer whistling hum of passing musket balls so shockingly near his ears.

He said, "It was Union infantry tree snipers and they tried blistering up on us mounted troopers. There was the sudden and ugly sound of ripping horse and human flesh, and the stink of sweat, blood, urine and…death. This blended with the shattering crash and crunch of ball on bone, chased by the cries of shear agony of man and beast alike. All of this entered my ears, the rifle reports followed onto the miserable demise of man and beast."

As Slim sat listening to the tale, he heard more hurt and anguish than he ever figured on knowing about in this life, or in any other life for that matter. In a trance like state Ornery told of his betrothed, a gal named Miss Charlotte O'Flynn, a young woman for whom he was well acquainted, badly fond of and recently engaged to. She was a fiery, much red-haired, petite, yet buxom speckle-breasted little lass of the

"Isles", that'd gone on an afternoon ride with him one day during the years of that war. And, of how she'd expired in his arms.

Ornery and she shared the same saddle mount after Charlotte's horse lamed up during their ride back to her home. In his southern cavalry First Sergeant's dress uniform and she in her engagement gown, and riding up in Ornery's lap seated just behind the saddle horn, Miss Charlotte was humming a sweet tune to him when a slapping sound struck her dress at the left breast abruptly halting her song. Her head turned toward Ornery, who for a flash was startled, a smile on her hushed lips. Charlotte gasped no breath, but died dead in his arms.

At that same instant Ornery, whose arms were wrapped around her waistline, felt warm blood flowing down onto his reign filled clasped hands. The blood ran down the front of her brilliantly textured emerald green dress, in stark contrast to all else. Ornery felt her heart burst up inside her with the projectile's impact, oddly enough, and he sensed her spirit rapidly depart from out of her evenly balanced saddle sat body.

Then, and only then did there follow the report of a musket washing over Ornery's startled ears, a shot from a very far off distance. Slim felt chills come over his body as Ornery told his story. He saw the terror and anguish in Ornery's eyes, just as if it were transpiring right then and there in the line shack at just that very moment.

With a brief pause and a sip from his drinking cup, Ornery continued telling his way around more equally gruesome stories of hostilities he encountered on the battlefields of yesteryear. He spake of the time he'd first came up against the Henry Repeating steel and brass-framed metallic-cartridge lever rifle. With that unfortunate battlefield introduction, the catastrophic experience none to fortuitous for his confederate compatriots; he shared how a whole bunch of them got shot to shreds by rifles that never ever seem to run out of ammunition during battle. Ornery grew more pale and lifeless with every tale.

Slim, in a switch of heart, wished he could've been there with Ornery and the good Captain in those days. On hearing Ornery's telling of Cap and his boys, Slim supposed he knew where much of the funning that Ornery had come up with now came from, and that he so generously dispensed upon Slim and others. Slim loved these stories very much, now pondering on how the Captain must have been a pleasure to be around, even when he, Slim, wasn't. On the spot that very night Slim decided he truly liked Captain Reed aplenty.

Ornery supposed the Captain was a man not much older than he, Ornery, was back then, probably twenty-three or four-years-old. He told how the Captain had a bold, stately, and courageous presents any place he was or done went. Captain Reed was an exceptionally fine horseman and marksman, too, who oft' killed game or adversaries from the back of his mount from extreme distances with regularity. He did this, to the amazement of his own men, time and time again.

Now Ornery clarified that Reed didn't do this for pleasure of bragging rights, but from grave necessity. Captain never dispensed his gifted talents for amusement, but for the purpose that was simply, war. More than that the Captain's ability to lead his outfit and safeguard his troopers through those trying times was why he existed at all. Lastly, the Captain didn't tolerate those who attempted to abuse and misuse his troopers either. He rapidly disabused that notion in many who tried doing so. He loved his God, his country, his family, his south, his soldiers and his calling. He had but one hate, war! And again, all was silent, save the light breeze whistling through the cabin frame and the low pitch of the fire rumbling in the cabin stove.

Slim started to speak when Ornery suddenly went to a storytelling fit, "The Captain strictly forbad us mistreatment or neglect of our mounts, equipment, weapons, each other, or even captives in our stead. He patiently demonstrated the proper detail guv to; the beasts, saddles, clothing, guns, and all that was to be upon his soldiers while at battle or not. By his orders and example every man did this caring themselves of their horse and gear, daily, before any of them fetched their own vittles or bedded down, down, usually on the cold damp ground. This, because he, and they, never knew when they might have to rise up and ride upon absolutely no notice, for this was the way it was in a 'go fast, ready to ride' outfit. It was the only way we continued to survive, day in and day out. His regimen of discipline and action saved us from undue casualties, certain decimation and death, time and time over."

Ornery stopped his gas and gab as Slim's ears caught Ornery's chuckle, and he spake of the time Captain and the boys were in a riding melee upon the rear and flank side of a Union artillery battery, "Now I'd shot my very first revolver of the fray dry and flung it aimlessly in to the clustered skirmishers as they withdrew from the lopsided engagement. The very next thing I witnessed was Cap jerking a revolver from the hand of a fellow adversary, a young Union lieutenant trying to take aim on me, as the Cap saber slashed the man's forearm off while fetching the same man's revolver. The Captain tossed the fully charged revolver to me, saying, 'Hang on to this one First-Sergeant, but if you do throw it, make sure you aim to do some damage, please.' Off he rode back into the fray fearless as ever. This proved Cap was more afraid of me dying for the lack of sufficiently maintained equipment than for loosing of his own soul. This happened all the time with that man, and not only for me."

Ornery shared that when they got in a hard place or overwhelming enemy counter-attacked, Cap would order him to punch a hole out and he'd handle a delaying action, putting himself in great danger. When we would finally arrive to our rally point Captain Reed would be the last one in, saving more troopers more oft' than he ever lost. Ornery offered, "And in the time I served with him, until I was transferred to

Tucker's command, he was ne'er struck or even nicked by nary a ball or bullet. Plum charmed was my opinion o' this man and his manner."

Ornery continued, "The Captain said, 'Rough and ready was ready to ride!' Make no mistake here, the Captain meant, 'fight' to be inclusive by the word 'ride'. Therefore, ready to ride and fight was his full implication. So it was; ride, fight, eat, sleep, and make ready to ride and fight, and that was all we did back then in 'em times o' that conflagration."

To hear Ornery tell it the Captain served at West Point Military Academy prior to the war, while others claimed he was a professor of engineering, chiefly a surveyor, assigned to Washington, D.C. However, the Captain was a private man and did never brag or make tell upon his subordinate colleagues none. As our leader he focused his attention on his duties, his orders, his immediate well-being, and us. Ornery figured him to be a professor of engineering, at the 'Point', until the division of the states, the military men and the war came. This much was certain; Captain Reed was truly a stalwart commander, remarkably fair and humanly decent. He knew his place in that war and did it plenty good and proper. He stood by us and we were, to a man, loyal to the bone to him without hesitation.

Finally, Ornery explained how many a poor fool, misguided friend, or honorable rival paid dearly for fooling about with our outfit's loyalty to the good Captain. Nonetheless, the same good Captain disallowed us from retaliation, revenge or foolish acts of careless disrespect and rare never was this disrespect guv by us. We well understood his manner and he never told us twice, never needed to.

Once more there was the making of a tear in Ornery's eye. Whatever happened to Captain Reed, well, Ornery never said for certain. While this didn't mean anything tragic had happened to the fine Captain, Slim didn't desire to further challenge Ornery's memories of the past, or to witness anymore of that grievously miserable war through Ornery's sad eyes that night.

As always and seemingly would be forever more for Ornery and Slim, much had to be done on the coming 'morrow. So's they cashed in for the night, Slim knew this much already. He'd learned much more then he'd bargained for from and about his older friend, and realized more than he wanted to know with just a single, seemingly, simple question or so he thought. However, as they settled into their bunks, peaceably, and beyond Slim's personal control, he blurted out, "So why didn't ya' ever go back to bein' schoolteacher after the war?"

"G'd NIGHT, Slim!" Ornery stated, blowing out the table lantern and going for his bunk. And, if they'd only half known what was coming next they'd never gotten out of beds ever again.

# Chapter VIII

## DR. GATLIN AND NAPOLEON'S CURE
## FOR AN UNWELCOME RAILROAD

Slim hadn't been on the ranch long that summer but he'd been around long enough to know when queer was a brewing on the place. By the looks of things it was trouble, plain and simple. His first clue was seeing his bunkie being called to the 'big house'. Hap, the fill in field *segundo* and Wyatt Kilpatrick, the wrangler were called there too. Then Cookie was called there, and it wasn't Christmas Eve when all such folks usually converged on the big house all at once, so said, Slim realized this queerness was for true. And, being it was only just August it was a mite early for Christmas Eve or even planning such a deal. Something was, in fact, amiss

Now them folk was all in there with Mr. Tucker and Cap'n Stewart for a fair lay of the morn' before they reappeared on the front porch. Slim was pouring pails of water in the trough up near the big house and heard them coming out. He over heard the Cap'n say something about, "fetchin' back a cure for 'em fools by the ways o' ol' Doc Gatlin!" This confused Slim since the doctor in town was, Doctor Bannon, not Gatlin. Slim didn't know of any other doctor about these parts by the name of Gatlin, a name he didn't recognize.

There was a light gray structure on the yard built completely of granite stone, except for the large heavy oak doors and heavy beamed roof. The edifice was totally devoid of windows and the only way in or out was through the big doors. It appeared Mr. Tucker spared no expense to build the blockhouse. Never much was said about the place called, *the li'l citadel.* A certain kind of secrecy hung over it. Slim had only ever been in the structure but one time to help Ornery fetch a case of cartridges out before they went to the hills some weeks back.

It was dark inside and they didn't tarry long before they were back outside. Slim thought he'd seen three objects; on wheeled carriages, tarped, and cloaked from view. The place was; very clean, orderly, cool, dry and filled with wooden boxes and crates, probably; tools, guns, powder, and ammunition Slim figured.

Now Slim stopped his chores and waited for Ornery to come his way. As Ornery approached, he wore a harsh countenance. Slim hadn't seen Ornery like this before and was curious to know what was going now.

"What's this hullabaloo all about, Ornery?" asked Slim, curiously.

"Those poor, sad, ignorant, greedy fools," Ornery's reply as he walked past Slim, like Slim wasn't even there. Ornery headed over to the bunkhouse. Looking around the big yard good, Slim spotted Kid and he set forth upon quick boot heels so's to make a connection with the cow detective and have sufficient words upon the matter of highly irregular situation.

"Howdy Kid," said Slim. What's afoot?"

"Death's comin' and all hell rides with Him!" answered Kid, as he walked past on his way to the li'l citadel, no joy showing on his face.

All the sudden Slim felt lonelier than a lone tumbleweed left out on the Texas prairie without a breeze he done guessed. He watched Ornery, Hap, Wyatt, and Sammy the cook, as went to their respective corners of the ranch. Each wore anger and disgust like an over stuffed packsaddle. Slim thought it felt like war was gonna bust loose at any time.

Slim turned back to his buckets and went about hauling water to and from the well pump to the nearby yard troughs. As he labored he began to watch about so's to see if'n he could figure out the mystery that was unfolding. As he watched, clues began to appear. First, a pair of chuck wagons came up to the cook shack. Second, two covered wagons appeared at the citadel and Ornery was driving one of the wagons. One by one the covered wagons took their turn going in and coming out of the secretive stone structure. Finally, a tarp covered limber or carriage piece was horse drawn out.

As Slim finished up watering the troughs he watched vigilantly as the yard began to fill up with a short wagon train. From a distance, up on the porch of the big house, Slim recognized Mr. Tucker and Cap'n Stewart a standing. He saw them wearing what appeared to be a light-gray colored, half-caped military fashioned bib tunic blouses and dark-gray trousers.

As Slim headed for the washhouse his curiosity was truly piqued by the unfamiliar commotion. Done up with this chore, Slim headed for the bunkhouse. When Slim came into the bunkhouse he met Ornery whose disposition was now his ol' Ornery self, whistling up a tune that sounded like a cavalry bugle call. Ornery heard Slim coming at him, Slim smiling that funny crooked smile. He motioned Slim to join him.

"Grab yer bedroll," said Ornery, "with these fresh togs and yer long lever gun. Weez got some weed pullin' to do, lad!" Slim stood there trying to read the tone in Ornery's voice while trying to marriage it to Ornery's words so's to fetch his meaning.

"What's goin' on here with all 'em wagons and 'em odd lookin' duds Mr. Tucker and the Cap'n are sportin'?" Slim asked. Ornery laughed and pointed them both for the bunkhouse door.

"That's General Tucker to ya', son," said Ornery, "and we're takin' a wagon train headed fer war, a range war with 'em confoundedly greedy and no good railroad barons!"

In his head Slim was still trying to solve this mystery and now he was even more confounded. Slim said softly, simply not seeing the whole picture fully, "General Tucker, wagon train, range war, and a no good railroad?" Ornery took Slim back into the bunkhouse and as they went he told Slim what he wanted to know. Ornery explicated how, during the war, Mr. Tucker had come to the rank of Brigadier General of the Army of the Confederated States. Cap'n Stewart had been a Lieutenant Colonel, Aide-de-Camp, to General Tucker.

After the war these two were among a very slim few select of southern military officers permitted to retain their commissions as Mr. Tucker had solid Yankee roots and was known goodly by the new Union General in the region. They were directly converted to the Union forces to aid the Texas border country into an orderly manner via the reconstruction of the southern states. The General and Lieutenant Colonel were ranked down to Colonel and Captain for a time before we all mustered out of military service and plum got gone out of Texas by the end of 1860's.

Ornery then told of how some skunky-bum railroad company out of Nebraska was trying to weasel their way across free grazing territory, like the O U T Spread and others spreads to link to some supposedly new east-west spur rail coming to Well Springs. Ornery said, "Well, that was just plain war, fer shore-n-fer certain." Mr. Tucker, the Cap'n, the old hands, and '*arbuckles*' of the outfit were gonna go and 'negotiate' directly with that twin steel rail skunk setup, straight up.

As for the light and dark gray togs Mr. Tucker and Cap'n were wearing, well it wasn't long before every man in the expedition was fashioned in like form, including Ornery and Slim. So Slim figured the words, 'negotiate' and 'war,' might well have meant the very same thing where they were headed. And, Ornery didn't dissuade that notion any none, either.

Mr. Tucker called on his neighbors over at the Twenty Spread to make these negotiations better balanced by the addition of more manpower. Slim recalled how the folks over at the Twenty Spread come by their handle. It was so named by the fact the outfit was started on a twenty-dollar bet, commenced going up the trail with only twenty head of Texas Longhorns, and was later manned by twenty cowhands, including the boss owner, Mr. James Hughes Pratt with ties to British Isles.

As Slim prepared his war bag and bedroll so's to put them both onboard the bedroll wagon and his saddle gear for the trail, his thoughts drifted toward Miss Denise and their, maybe, never future. He knew Mr. Tucker would not do anything brassy, or fool-hearty, with his outfit, yet he'd do what it took to stave off commercial or industrial tomfoolery. How-some-ever, Slim wasn't certain he was up for getting 'whacked down in some fool up range dispute between cows and 'choo-choo's'. Nevertheless, no one had forced him at gunpoint to sign on with the O U T Spread and he was part of the herd for better or worse. So he was headed for war when all he truly wanted was to go visit his much favorite-d calico, Miss Denise.

Smiling, Ornery queried, "Ya' gonna…" Slim jumped, startled from his daydream… "stare holes in that war bag or fill it up?" Slim rapidly stuffed the remaining set of trousers in his bag and cinched bag closed.

"Weez goin' to town before we git to this campaign?" Slim asked shyly.

"Nope," Ornery replied, "the county sheriff was near kill't and his short posse nigh on run off by 'em railroad skunks. So the General said we'd go straight away and make 'peace' or 'pieces' on the lower range o' our Spread!" Slim nodded as he took hold of his saddle gear and bag. War it was, so's he reckoned, and if'n there was time he'd go visit his favorite gal in town, if'n he survived all this.

Within the hour General Tucker's outfit was formed up in a double horse column, along with the wagons and limber in tow, and going forth from 'fort headquarters' or the big house. They were headed to the most southern border of the Spread to meet the railroad surveying team.

The General and his Captain called the troopers to move out, leading the column away going east by south to discover the adversary.

Some time later and quite unexpectedly Kid rode up along side Slim, who was in the column next to Ornery, just two horses back from the lead. Kid handed Slim a yellow ribbon wrapped envelop. Hand scribed on this envelop in indigo ink was a single word, "*SLIM*", he recognized the hand script straight up, it was his, Miss Denise. After Kid handed Slim the ribbon wrapped envelop, he smiled, nodded to Slim, and rode away, south from the column and disappeared over the rise and gone.

"Where's he off to?"

"Off to do da job he's hired on to do," answered Ornery. Slim detected a hint of secrecy so he figured he didn't want to know no more. He was, however, grateful for the letter delivery. Slim wondered how Kid managed to get that letter from Miss Denise so swiftly. Perhaps he'd ask Kid later, if'n later ever came, and he lived that long. The column plodded along and Slim's brand new wool tunic itched on him something fierce as such, and he was dying to loose it off, if'n he only could.

"Ornery," Slim asked, "how come weez have to wear the same ol' tunics and trouser, like weez some kinda army er somethin'?" Ornery smiles at Slim and replied, "Ya' er some kinda army here today."

"I thought we're jus' cowmen o' the O U T."

"There's yer first problem, ya' thought," said Ornery, "an' ya' are a cowman, but think o' it this way, ya' want Rafe or Kid ta hole ya' in the bread basket or the head?" Wide-eyed, Slim shook his head. Then Ornery spake it way, "Well then, just make derned good and shootin' sugar sure ya' look like one o' the general's troopers an' ya'll live longer, *comprende usted*, er ya' understand?" Ornery eyed a big smile on Slim's face, as Slim totally un-disremembered that the new woolen tunic collar and cuffs was pestering him on his neck and wrists.

He thought Mr. Tucker…General Tucker was a wise man to work for, for he thought of everything that was fair and proper for his cow-troopers. So their day went on, both saddlers plum pleasured to be done of it for the day when it was all over.

At mid-afternoon, the day next, orders were passed to the outfit to halt and set up camp. When camp was set up, Slim marveled at how much the camp resembled a military bivouac so he supposed from photographs he'd seen in old newspapers from when he was a young boy. He also noticed that the longer his bunkie was on campaign the less tight was his disposition. Ornery just pleasured in jawing about the olden days, back during that 'derned' war as he so oft' referred to it.

Seemingly all the old hands like; Mr. Tucker, Cap'n Stewart, Hap, Sammy, Charlie, old Fletch, and Ornery were plenty pleasured to be back on campaign. What's more, Slim noticed the old hands fussed over the two covered wagons and the caisson and limber wagon. He also noted how the elders kept the young cowhands busy away from them. He hadn't been able to get even Ornery to fess up about the particular-ness of those wagons.

There were plenty of chores to do and the new saddlers were guv to them. They were to fetch in the fuel for the campfires, the water, dig privies, and tend to the horses and the mules. As the sun went set Slim sensed the coming day was going to be the appointed day for which they'd come all this way for.

Slim pondered a spell before he engaged Ornery in conversation so's to learn more of what was coming up, asking, "Ornery, what's gonna happen again' us tomorrow?" Ornery sensed the concern in Slim's tone and the trepidation etched on the young man's face.

"Ya' just pleasure yerself with that letter ya' got from Miss Ellington and just do what Cap'n Stewart or I tell ya' to do. Ya'll do fine as the frog's hair, okay?" Once more Slim nodded customarily much wondering what 'frog hair' had to do with what anything they was to be doing on futuristically. Ornery told him to go check his gear one last time and get to bed, and that's what Slim did.

Ornery headed up to main camp to join leadership before he took his turn at perimeter watch on horseback. As he came to camp he thought of how much this reminded him of the days of yesteryear. Also, of young men he used to know, back then, their faces now much older.

His heart went out to the young cowpunchers, like Slim, Tommy and Wyatt, and how they must have been feeling tonight, and not knowing quite how to feel. Ornery took his instructions and headed off to post his watch, then to bed late that night.

Slim eyed with delight the pastel fan of colors in the early morning skylight. He filled his lungs with the rich aroma of the dew laden prairie flowers and grasses as he sat his saddle. Slim peered down the wide valley that was camp; the light green grass, the pale white ducking canvas wall command tents, a long row of beige lean to covers, with bedrolls, and a newly erected pole, complete with a Confederate-States battle flag. Knowing, from what he'd heard told, that symbol of rebellion may well call down grave consternation with the 'Federals' should they find it. Now this flag was either Cap'n Stewart's or Ornery's idea, but it flew on Mister Tucker's property by his guv consent. For all of this, he was certainly pleasured his watch was over. Slim rode past the main campfire up to where his lean to was and turned in for some much appreciated shut-eye.

Hours later Slim was startled from his slumber by a single gunshot. He was on his feet and gazing around over the top of his lean to cover. Tommy Gardner on top of the south rim, on watch, had fired that signal shot from his '72 Colt 'Open-Top' revolver. The boys mounted their ponies and galloped up the slight slope to the south ridge, and to Tommy.

Mr. Tucker, Cap'n Stewart, and Hap joined Tommy and the boys there. There they caught first sight of the party they'd all been waiting on. It was the railroad survey team. This party was comprised of two, four-horse drawn box wagons and eight mounted riders. They'd come to survey, stake and rail track grade the prairies of Tucker's spread. This was something Mr. Tucker was not going to abide by and planned to put a swift end to.

Tucker's camp sprang to life as Slim hurried to clad up in his issued togs and got to Pete, his pony and made ready to ride to join the rest of the party there. As Slim reached the south ridge top and dismounted. He stood gazing in near disbelief of what he saw. On Cap'n Stewart's orders, Fletch Thompson and his gun crew uncovered their field piece and positioned it. When he saw the brass cannon Slim began to figure out just how real this conflict truly was and why the oldsters was so originally displeasured.

Ornery rode up from the east and hastily explained Slim to the goings on and that he, Slim, would be tending the horse band with the horse boss, Wyatt. Then Ornery headed west as Slim headed to fetch some grub and go find the horse boss, a fellow just a bit older than he by a year or so.

Meanwhile, Cap'n Stewart and his delegation of three riders rode out to meet the survey team. They trotted three hundred and fifty yards south to negotiations. When Slim reached the top of the south ridge he found Wyatt and saw the survey party, wagons, and more. He also noticed that the outfit's covered wagons were sitting on the outer edge of the low running east-west lip of the ridgeline, rears facing south pointed in the direction of survey teams. Slim paid his courtesies to the General; then Wyatt and he took to the horse band up behind the supply point.

The survey party turned their wagons about and departed south, back to their main frontier made camp miles away. The war looked to be over, finally, until Cap'n Stewart and his party returned to camp. He reported to Mr. Tucker that all was not well. The Cap'n shared that the tone of the negotiations lead him to strongly believe the railroad, used to having its way by hook or crook, wasn't going to be run out of this territory by a handful of seemingly errant cattlemen.

So Mr. Tucker corralled his bosses at the main headquarters tent to work up the next stage of what appeared to be an unavoidable battle between the cowmen and the choo-choo men as Slim like to call them. Slim was pleasantly pleased when he spotted Rafe and Kid coming from the headquarters tent. He was certain they were in the 'field', but so was he for that matter. Slim headed their way.

"Where'd ya' two come from?" Slim queried.

"Outta the grass and off the hills," replied Kid. Slim didn't really follow his meaning, but figured he'd not push for an answer if'n it wasn't guv to him plain. Kid said to Slim, "Be ready to ride with me before first light, weez some company business to do for Tucker." Slim wondered what was up now.

"Do Wyatt, Ornery and Cap'n Stewart know this?"

"Yep, who'd ya' think assigned ya' to me."

"Good enough fer me." The two men parted ways as Slim headed to locate Ornery so's to learn more.

He found Ornery on the south ridge with the cannon and its crew. It was that cannon once again that fetched Slim's attention, full up. It was the one that Ornery had described as cast by *Leeds and Co.*, a brass 'twelve-pounder' with a seventy-two inch barrel, weighing nigh on 1,220 lbs., and a lethal weapon in the hands of an experienced artillery gun crew.

Just as the General requested and was the war plan, the cannon had just been charged with a shell load, aimed and ranged for a wear spot in the grassy plain some four hundred and fifty yards away. Slim headed to where the cannon was positioned and immediately saw and felt the flashing "KA-B-O-O-O-M!" of the field piece. A few long moments later, "B-A-L-A-A-M," the shell exploded. Smoke and dirt reeled into the air as the ball hit its target spot directly. A heavy blanket of whitish-blue smoke covered the field where the Napoleon brass cannon now rested.

Slim welled up with excitement as he rode toward Ornery. It seemed that all was set with the outfit's artillery. All of this just in case trouble did return in the form of railroad men, their horses and wagons and their guns. Slim rode up to Ornery's spot, puzzled, "What's ya' shootin' that field piece at and why?" Ornery pointed to a spot some 450 yards away, "That grass patch out there, the one with a cannon ball hole in the middle of it. And as we're to doin' the biddin' o' the boss, an' none more." The bunkies conversed a spell and Slim turned his pony back around for camp.

Slim knew he'd best be to getting back to camp to readying himself for the job Kid and he had coming in the morning. Yet, out of pure child-like curiosity Slim had to scrutinize old Fletch Thompson's cannon crew for what it was doing, as they recharged their tube. He rode up and sat a spot three yards away to peer on. Slim recognized the gun crew as; Fletch, Sack Thomas, Petee Mac, and Benny Wilson as they'd already rolled the cannon back into its previous firing position by the time Slim settled into observe.

First, the cannon crew situated the gun as Fletch took to cleaning up the cannon's vent hole on the top rear of the barrel with an odd looking small bristled brush. He pocketed the brush and with a gloved left hand covered up the vent hole.

Second, Sack was right there with the worm tool, a tool that looked like a rake handle with a short, huge overgrown compressed corkscrew on the end, to 'worm' or scrape out the back or base of the gun bore.

He snaked it about and worked it to and fro 'til he was certain that no more debris was left in the bore innards.

Third, Pete came right along with wet mop, which was a water moist, tight fitting mop of lamb's wool. He rammed and rotated his mop down the cannon's inside a pair of goes, or twice.

Fourth, beings the bore was clean, Benny came right behind Pete with the dry mop, as Fletch observed, along with Slim, every move his crew was doing and swiftly to boot. Benny repeated Pete's action, basically, so's to dry and clean the inside of the barrel, and prepared it ready for a powder charge.

Fifth, Pete stowed his mop and fetched up a pre-measured and pre-wrapped powder charge within a canvas bag, never actually touching the paper-wrapped powder charge itself. He carefully set it inside the muzzle end of the cannon mouth milking it out of the canvas cover avoiding the paper canister by human touch of his moist hands, being mindful not to place himself in front of the muzzle directly. Fletch watched on. Pete stowed his wet mop on the limber rack and took hold of the long 'J' shaped ramming tool to set the charge in, down and tightly to the base of the barrel. This hook headed tool permitted the charge to be sent into the tube without placing a soul, with ramming tool, straight in front of the muzzle, along side the tube while it was being charged. Pete finished setting the powder charge bundle to the back of gun, seating it good and tight.

Sixth, the projectile was carefully placed and rammed tightly aft against the set powder charge. Slim noted how each man stayed clear of the muzzle end while doing his very task in close quarters to the gun muzzle.

With the loading finished, Fletch removed his gloved hand from the flash hole. With the crew clear of the muzzle, he pulled on a leather laced string around his neck until he found the gimlet, a wood handled awl like pick tool and set it over the opening of the flash hole. He guv it a grand tap on the top end until he felt the sharp metal end strike down and puncture the tightly packed powder charge beneath the flash hole. Fletch called, "Primer," and Sack gingered his setting of that fiction primer into the flash hole, its brass looped head protruding from the flash-hole top.

Fletch and his team ascertained that the gun was still set in place, in battery, to shoot and properly targeted. Fletch asked Slim to move further away and looked to Cap'n Stewart, who in turn nodded. After he nodded to Fletch, Fletch carefully drew up the slack the stringed lanyard cord, gripping the small wood handle in his left hand, and carefully hooking the opposite end into the brass loop on the friction primer. Cautiously, Fletch stepped right and away from the barrel and wheel parts of the cannon's rear right flank, a gentle slack remained in his lanyard. He looked around at his crew, his gun, down range, and back to the crew. He nodded at Cap'n and the Cap'n shouted, "FIRE!"

In nigh on a split second, "KA-B-O-O-O-M," roared the cannon. A huge field of blue-gray smoke rushed forth, as the gun wheeled itself rearward away from the cannoneer*, his crew, in a spectacular eruption of flame.

With that, a projectile, now racing at some eight hundred miles an hours, flew out to its intended target and exploded on point. It was a spectacle to behold. Slim turned his pony about and rode back to main camp, as the crew set to repeat their drill again. Slim pondered what it would be like to see this piece used against man and beast. He hoped maybe that it wouldn't have to come in a swift blink of an eye, this machine against man and beast. Slim was pleasured by the moment as he witnessed such activity. And as their day wound down to a close, Ornery, Slim and the rest of the outfit settled in for another night, not truly knowing what tomorrow would bring and who'd die, if any.

Before first light, Kid and Slim rode out of camp going north and east. Rafe and Donny Quirt, of the Double X, rode north and west. Large pots of belly wash were kept going on the fire pit by Cookie all night and day, and Ornery filled his cup for the sixth time as he did his perimeter ride about camp on watch.

Later, he rousted the boys from their bedrolls to their saddles and their chores, before the daylight got on them good. Breakfast was hardly done up when a signal shot rang out from the lookout point, where the Napoleon field piece stood covered. A flurry of cowmen scampered to their ponies and galloped to the ridge top, the cannon and to the lookout point to witness the fresh commotion.

The revolver report startled Slim from his daydream. Kid snickered at Slim's reaction, from where they both lay in the tall grass, in hiding. Kid nodded in the direction of the party of riders and wagons coming north up a cow trail.

Kid carefully glassed the company through his brass glass-filled eyepiece. He knew Rafe was doing the very same thing from a point rather due west of him over a half mile away. Kid counted four mule drawn wagons and fifty horse riders coming north toward the O U T boys. It was that railroad party once more. Slim aided Kid, as Donnie helped Rafe. Rafe and Kid were there, well, to be 'snakes-in-the-grass', or to dissuade enemy activity with long guns that is, should the need arise. Kid knew that Mr. Tucker had set his defense perimeter well inside the ranch property line so's there would be no mistake that these railroad folk come bearing ill will. So ready these two cow detectives would be in support and in the defense of their home and herd.

As a gesture of good will and under the ordered of the boss, Ornery and Roy Covington of the O U T, and Pat Johnson and Billie Sims of the Double X prepared to ride out under a white flag to negotiate, again, with the railroad team. Sadly, the railroad didn't choose to abide by the words Cap'n Stewart had spake to them the day before. Now Ornery's party was gonna get them to understand or else.

Cap'n ordered the cannon charged and aimed, just in case. As that took place Ornery's party rode forth to meet the railroad. The two special covered wagons were sent out to positions on the lower ridge face flanking the artillery piece. Slim pondered about them wagons, but didn't desire to disturb Kid with conversation about their purpose.

In the meantime, Rafe and Kid watched, peaceably, from their grassy knoll perches, Sharps long rifles set on cross-sticks, steady, loaded and ready. Kid spied intently as the two parties met in the great distance far off. He reckoned his bullet was two, two and a half seconds away, should he have to send one at the first sign of trouble. Rafe was no closer on the west side of field still. All seemed to be set for peace or for war, but it was difficult to say which at this point. The peace hung in the balance as Kid sat quietly, praying silently for peace to prevail, gripping his rifle in case of war.

General Tucker and the Cap'n Stewart observed by field glasses from the ridge, where a two-dozen mounted cowmen and a cannon crew watched and waited and wondering patiently. It was difficult to discern exactly what was happening at the negotiations.

Then something queer appeared to happen between the cowmen and railroaders. Through their field glasses they watched on as some revolver steel suddenly flashed, appearing in the hands of the railroad men. Riders and horses appeared nervy at that very same gathering of souls. A mounted rider from the railroad survey team pulled and leveled a lever rifle in the direction of Ornery and his party. Kid spotted Ornery jerking his revolver, he spake a swear word under his breath, loud enough to draw Slim's attention again. He carefully tugged the rear trigger, his set trigger, and ever so gently touched the front trigger of his Sharps Model '74 long rifle, the one in caliber, .45-110, it spake authoritatively,

"K-A-A-WOOM!"

Kid's rifle barked out, the smoke and flame discharged forth, as the mighty paper-patched, heavy lead 523-grain projectile hurled speedily out to his target. In a double long moment the man, the one with the rifle barrel pointed at Ornery, his body flinched, a bright crimson color spewed forth from the unannounced puncturing long flown projectile. The shock of the lead bullet ripped into his right ribbed torso. As the man's body absorbed the shock of Kid's bullet, the lever gun was unsettling from his grasp. Unexpectedly the sound of Kid's rifle shot was awash over the whole valley. The war was on and there was li'l or no chance of peace now.

Rapidly all lead hail busted loose between the two parties; the four lead by Ornery and a line of the railroaders at Ornery's front. Ornery and Pat swiftly cut their ponies hard left, turned back headed for the outfit's covered wagon on their right. Roy and Billie cut their horses in the opposite manner, riding away swiftly for the other O U T covered wagons. Dust, smoke, and hot lead greeted their hasty retreat, straight away, laying flat against their ponies for concealment from the shooters at their backs.

Almost instantly General Tucker nodded his permission and Cap'n Stewart shouted to the cannoneer, "Fire!" In a blink Fletch Thompson yanked the long lanyard cord attached to the friction primer and the cannon boomed out the first blast of the day.

Immediately the cannon team set to reload of their wheeled gun. As the gun was wheeled back in position, its projectile struck its mark. The first tarpaulin covered wagon erupted in a wild explosion that sorely confounded every man and beast within seventy yards. Here, Ornery, Pat, Roy and Billie got the break they badly needed so's to get from harm's way.

Rafe and Kid set to bide their time shooting down one, and then another of the hired railroad men or anyone who raised a gun against the punchers. Slim and Donnie stayed ready to aid their pards should they need to make a swift'ed retreat, if'n they were found out. Rafe and Kid plied their long gun trade on the encroacher swiftly as; Ornery, Pat, Roy, and Billie finally arrived at the canvas-covered wooden destinations. As they did the railroad 'army' recovered from the first shell blast and set into motion their horse-mounted counter-attack against the O U T and Double X boys.

Time, blood and smoke told, and it wasn't long before Kid and Slim was found out for their rifle handy work on the surveying team. Soon a dozen railroad riders formed up and took to riding down Kid and Slim's grassy hideout, some two hundred and fifty yards away.

In the mean time, Ornery climbed up in the wagon and joined up on Charlie Spragg. They rapidly peeled back the rear canvas cover of their wagon as incoming bullets sped past Kid and Slim like a freshly stirred hornet's nest. Ornery steadied up and let fly with his Gatlin gun crank handle. He aimed to lead that bunch going at Slim and Kid as it took a few short bursts to find his range and aim point.

"Pow-pow-pow… pow-pow… pow-pow-pow… pow-pow-pow-pow-pow," spake the rotating ten-barreled gun. Pat pointed out to where Kid and Slim were. Ornery deliberately took extra time to line up his gun. Charlie fed the gun a fresh stick magazine of forty shiny brand new long rifle cartridges as Ornery rotated the gun's crank handle.

As he did, both horse and riders were cut down dead in a most lethal manner via the big powerful 45-70 hunks of flying lead projectiles. Pat called out targets and affect for Ornery while Charlie kept the gun full of ammo as Ornery fired his gun with astonishing effectiveness. As they worked to preserve the lives of Kid and Slim from certain death, a new mounted party, not ready to quit up the fray, rode swiftly toward Ornery and crew, their guns blazing away.

Chunks of wood from Ornery's wagon and pieces of lead from the incoming bullets were flying ever-which-a-way as chips and splinters on Ornery's crew. As they stood making their defense in and under the wagon, Ornery steadied up his gun's aim and rate of fire. With a gentle sweep to and fro, he kept it pointed amidst of the partially smoke obscured attackers. This formation began to scatter as the gun smoke became so dense Ornery couldn't accurately distinguish a real solid point of aim upon the group of galloping assailants.

Seeing this second group; shooting, shouting and hauling down on Ornery's Gatlin gun wagon, Kit Allison, Ray, and Billie sprang into action from their wagon with the second Gatlin gun, with fatal effect.

As Pat's bullet nicked ear filled with sound of the hot pieces of lead wing passed, he looked to see his position coming under sustained assault by a bunch of railroading regulators. He swift-ed his way back to and under the gun wagon where he hoisted up and shouldered his lever gun to contribute to his own defense.

Kit and Billie kept their multi-barreled rotary gun working in concert with Ornery's piece. As Ornery fired on point to the incoming attack, Kit poured hot lead into railroader's long left flank, and in less than a minute this new and miserably murderous field of fire hacked down that threat rather efficiently. The intense pall of smoke lay heavy round about the two gun wagons as they both ceased fire, momentarily, so's to get a take of their situation with the enemy and their wits.

Ornery stood ready at the gun; Charlie fetched more cartridge sticks for their gun from the box on the wagon floor. Pat brought a pail of water from the barrel mounted on the wagon's left flank. He carefully poured it over the gun barrels and the internal cooling pad, the one up inside, beneath the ten barrels.

The General sat atop this copper colored, seventeen-hand high Dun gelding and surveyed the ensuing skirmish with his eyepiece. He was filled with anger and with pride as he observed the battlefield before him. He was plenty pleasured to see how well their plan was executing against the encroachers. Also by the way his cowmen-troopers were affecting the opposing force. However he had not wanted it to come down to this, an open melee of bloodshed between the two sides.

His Gatlin gun teams appeared victorious and secure unto themselves for the moment, anyway. Both dispatch shooters, Rafe and Kid, were still secure and working very effectively against the foe before them. His single cannon battery and main camp party was ready to exact a maximum response, now, so's to affect a swift and sure victory with minimal causalities. Mr. Tucker did however ponder what the Federal response might be to this, if any. Yet, more over, he was truly praying for a signal of capitulation, surrender as it were, from the railroad men, for his heart wasn't into this kind of play.

He observed the opposing force as they rallied to their wagons and he knew what needed be done. He rode to Cap'n Stewart; they surreptitiously conferred for a time. Cap'n directed the cannon crew to acquire a certain target and fire on it. And, the strategy was set to commence.

At the blast of the cannon nigh on everyone on the battlefield took note, probably nobody more so than the railroad boys for which it was meant. Both Gatlin gun wagons started firing at the large box wagon targets that could be acquired from their locations now that they'd freshly run out of mounted targets. The remaining mounted riders began to scatter from their formation to avoid, both, the cannon fire and the withering rounds from the deadly Gatlins. The cannon ball arched out to its target and exploded alongside the second and tallest mule drawn wagon of the wagon train. The blast caused the second wagon to reel over on its side, in pieces, and burst into flame.

As it did, Kit tore into it with his Gatlin gun as fire spread swiftly around it and onto the third wagon. As the third wagon caught fire, the remaining wagon and nearby mounted riders rapidly scattered in every direction under sun at breakneck speed.

The teamster* perched a top the third wagon hastily whipped his team into a steady full out run. In self defense he heaved himself from the now southbound runaway wagon. This wagon barreled away from the battle and the ensuing fight began to resemble a mass dispersion among the members of railroad party. Wagons, horses and riders scattered like seeds in a windstorm, in all four directions. As the wind fanned the fire of that wagon it spread to its load.

The shooting had stopped, as had the fighting in most places. The railroad boys were in an all fire hurry, a dead run, in to be anywhere but where that third wagon was. They knew the content of the wagon, and it didn't take long for the boys of the Double X and the O U T to figure out what was about to commence as well. The General and Cap'n braced themselves as did their outfit. The seconds counted down like minutes as the cowmen observed the ferocity of movement and mayhem on the battlefield in surreal time. With a sudden prolonged deafening roar-like pitch, the wagon and team whole disappeared into forever with a monumental thunderous multi-moment explosion and a massive monstrous fireball of dynamite, blasting caps and wood, lots of wagon and crate wood.

During that horrendous explosion folk were throwed down hard; objects were overturned, tossed, turned about and ripped and twisted apart totally. For quite a time bits and pieces of all shapes and sizes rained down from the clear blue sky. And, over hundreds of yards round from where the wagon had last been glimpsed the stuff came out from the heavens in a rain storm of debris.

Debris landed nigh on to where Ornery was and even where both Kid and Slim had been hole up. Not only did the dynamite blast the wagon to kingdom come, it also blasted the fighting spirit out of the railroad men too, just as General Tucker and the Cap'n had hoped for and took witness of. Swiftly, from the far off front, the men of the railroad were waving a white rag of capitulation and raised their hands in surrender.

On orders from the General, Cap'n Stewart and Dutch Hammond, *segundo* of the Double X were dispatched forward to take the terms of absolute surrender from the railroaders. Two-dozen cowpunchers joined up with the two *segundos*, as their mounted security detachment, in the acquiring of this surrender party.

The General sat his Dun and again observed the action from his south rim perch. He was now truly pleasured the skirmishing had finally abated, at least for now. As he glassed the field his heart sank as he witnessed so much human and animal carnage mixed with the sight and odor of gun smoke, and the stench of the burning wagons. The stink of death was plenty thick through the air for certain at that moment, and some time thereafter.

To the General's grand surprise he heard a gay commotion and the sound of women's voices from a distance to his rear. He turned to catch sight of the county sheriff, Porter Seaton. The sheriff was accompanied by a small party that including; Doc. Bannon, Mr. Pratt, Miss Ellington, Miss Emory, and a young lady-miss he simply didn't recognize, and other men and wagons in support of the O U T Spread.

Turning control of the once battlefield to his immediate adjutant, the General turned his horse and attention to the new arrivals so's to render a proper camp greeting, beings who they was and on how far they'd ventured to join him.

As mid-afternoon came on, the battle was over and patching up commenced about the battlefield on what once was a peaceful patch of O U T prairie grass. Aided by the company of the newly arrived calicos, lawmen and the doctor, the cowmen and railroad men toiled to care for the wounded and ailing *companeros* and their beasts.

Mr. Tucker finally received the capitulation accord he'd sought from the railroad from the very beginning. This, thanks to the railroad man, Mr. Samuel Chenoweth, and the sheriff, finally. The accord papers were signed, made official and turned over to Sheriff Seaton for delivery to the county courthouse recording office, at Well Springs. This settled it once and for all, this land-tract and rail track dispute.

Later the same day both the railroaders and cattlemen took to the miserably sad chore of taking care of the departed men, dead horses, and destroyed equipment. This chore would take up the rest of the day. Cap'n Stewart and Phil Barton, Mr. Chenoweth's foreman, saw to the clean up and the keeping of further peace between their respective crews.

The railroad outfit had gotten beaten up pretty soundly, with a bit better than half of them as casualties, being injured, wounded and outright killed down. The joint outfits, the combined Twenty and O U T Spreads had faired the wrangle splendidly, having only half dozen cow-troopers shot up a bit. Two of the O U T saddlers injured were Slim and his partner for the day, the Yellowstone Kid. Fortunately, theirs only minor bullet wounds. Slim suffered an ankle flesh wound and Kid a nasty scalp wound. Slim fixed up swell and soon. Kid bled a fierce mess and looking much worse that it actually was. He was left with harshly blurred vision and a really mean headache.

As Kid and Slim came back into camp from their prairie grass hiding post, it was the brand new gal's face that Kid had never glimpsed before that greeted them at the makeshift hospital tent. The calico face that took him by disconcerted surprise was the one and only, Miss Brennan. Miss Lisa Annette Brennan was for sure the recently posted schoolmarm of Well Springs. Her countenance was gentle mannered and with perfume that caused Slim to un-disremember the ribbon-wrapped letter he still had in his saddlebags that he'd yet to peer upon.

Once inside the tent Slim fetched a block of wood from a corner of the tent to make a sitting spot for his indignant pard. Kid stood a moment patiently waiting for Slim to bring him up a sit. As he stood there the schoolmarm peered on this wounded saddler at her front and took stock of who he was, and what ailed him. Also, she took note that Kid stood an inch shy of six foot tall, wore a lean look, and not a hundred and fifty pounds. He wore a head of shoulder long curly blonde locks and may have been mistaken for another version of a younger Colonel Custer, perhaps.

Kid oft' wore dusky hue colored attire, but not today as he was clad in his blood-stained light and dark gray, O U T issued, war garb. Miss Brennan set her gentle hands to unwrap Kid's hastily banded up head wound and began washing away all the dried blood so Doc Bannon could finish mending on him. He was pleasured for her gentleness and her calico-like carefulness. Yet this day he was wore down and some done in and found it difficult to make idle conversation with the nurse-teacher. He'd not a nights sleep in nearly three days for all his riding and hiding in the prairie grasses with his long gun. As she washed the dried blood from his face she smiled and Kid returned her kindness with a smile of his own. She seemed like an angel to him and an angel was plain and simply a rare occurrence in his life, ever.

Slim quietly hobbled away from that couple and out of the hospital tent. Once outside he took note of how the evening was over taking camp. Slim stopped just outside the tent flap, by a tent support pole, to rest his weary eyes for a moment. In a hard daydream Slim nearly leapt from his togs when a gentle hand tapped him on the right shoulder. He whirled about in place in time to discover Miss Denise standing just outside of the hospital's tent flap door next to him.

Slim could hardly believe his blurry and tired eyes as he glimpsed her straight up. He was so taken aback and pleasured to see his darling as he didn't realized she was even in camp because of his absence from camp all of that day. Slim reached out to her, took her hand, and pulled her to him in a tight embrace. They stood many long minutes together, silently, outside the tent door in a firmly embracing pose. Miss Ellington looked up into Slim's face, with a smile.

"You're surprised to see me here, aren't you?" queried Miss Denise.

"Uh…Yep," replied Slim, hesitantly.

"Didn't you receive my correspondence from Kid?"

"I did, I just ne'er got about to readin' it just quite yet. I am so very pleasured yer here, though. When ja' come to camp?"

"I came with the doctor this afternoon to aid the injured and I'm so pleasured to be here with you, too, and find you nigh on whole. I just came from the field where I was doing triage on the wounded there for the doctor." Then they went back inside the tent turned hospital.

Later, around the campfire, Mr. Tucker inquired of Mr. Chenoweth to the name of the teamster that had sacrificed his wagon and team to save everyone on the battlefield earlier, and if'n he was still on this side of the sod? Mr. Chenoweth inquired into the matter and was presented with one, Arnie Pole, teamster, who a bit beat up from his self-induced tumble from that wagon earlier.

The General was well pleased to meet Arnie and commenced to make good upon his earlier selfless act of courage with honor. He shared in words what many already knew in their heads that Arnie could have well rode his wagon into the forward battlefield, or nearer, and risked killing so very many men and more on both sides. Instead, he chose to ride away to the south to spare the lives of everyone on that battlefield. Mr. Tucker said, for all to hear, "If Arnie ever's mistreated by the railroad folks or if he ever grew tired of laboring for the railroad, he could always come be a part his O U T Spread, anytime." The boys of the O U T and Twenty Spreads let go a big "Hooray!" showing their concurrence.

Later the camp settled down for the night and all went well, even until the morn', when the twin parties prepared to strike camp and go their separate ways. Mr. Tucker left behind sundry supplies, water, and a pair of wagon for Mr. Chenoweth's men to journey back to their headquarters.

After five days the cow-troopers of both Spreads, their calico company, the law and Doc, set off on their way going home; first to the *ranchos* for some, and to town for the rest. Ornery was pleasured to discover the company of Miss Shannon, once he was back from helping secure his Gatlin gun wagons. With Ornery there, Miss Ellington made the polite point of introducing the schoolmarm around to the folks who'd yet to make her proper acquaintance. She was graciously received by all, and by no one more than Kid, as he recalled her special kindness and medical support to him, earlier.

As they formed up to trail back home, Slim found himself riding next to bandaged up Kid, trailing behind the surrey of the doctor and the gals. The two rode together, subdued in spirit, cuz of the events of the past days. Slim was in heavy though and turned his attention to Kid. He asked, "Does this fightin' stuff happen oft' around here Kid?" Kid replied with little emotion, "As oft' as it does." Slim took small comfort in Kid's answer for it didn't seem to answer his question whatsoever. He hoped for a more definitive response like; "last year" or "this was the third time in ten years". Slim said, "Ya' ever do this before, Kid?" Kid asked, "Ya' mean kill men with guns? And, no, not since the last time I had too." Slim swift recollected that either he wasn't asking the question properly, or that he wasn't gonna get a straight answer. This learning of the cow craft was a tricky trade at best and not cuz of the cows, but cuz of the men in charge of the cows.

After a moment Slim asked of Kid, "How'd ya' manage to git that note from the nurse before went on campaign?" Kid said, "I was commissioned to town where she guv it to me before I came to the ranch and we went to goin' to meet the railroad. That suit yer confoundedness?" Slim nodded and then his face was covered with a queer look of bewilderment as he turned to peer at Kid. Kid looked on with curiosity. Slim queried him, "If'n there wasn't any mountains, hills, trees or large rock obstacles between here and Well Springs, why was the railroad surveyin' team haulin' so much blasted dynamite?" About now Ornery rode up to Kid and Slim and heard Slim's question. Ornery nodded to Kid and Kid smiled back, his head still nagging him from his head wound some asked, "Would ja' agree they'd be wantin' to use dynamite to clear a path from here to town?" Slim nodded and Ornery smiled, knowing what was about to come out from Kid's mouth. In a true tone of certainty Kid answered, "Well Slim, 'em jaspers would use lots o' dynamite ta clear as many obstacles such as; ranch houses, corrals, line shacks, barns, cabins, water wells, and most o' all, we cowmen, our cows, and our way o' life."

Now Ornery piped up, "*Veni, vidi, vici,* Slim, my version of Julius Caesar Latin for, 'we came, we saw, and we conquered' and I sorely hope ya' took note o' how Mr. Tucker and our neighbors rode down the uninvited 'skunks'. He's a prudent, wise, courtesy, good hearted boss and all. But if'n folk come at his outfit, dirty and sideways, well, he'll put his 'brand' on 'em, if'n ya' know what I mean." Slim inquired, "Doctor Gatlin and ol' Napoleon sure can slap that brand on an unwelcome railroad, and don'cha believe, Ornery?" Ornery smiled back as the rest of the O U T boys burst out, "HOORAH!" Lots of lofty laughter followed.

Kid told how he and some boys, while delivering a band of horses, shot up the locomotive stack to ruin for the engineer was being cantankerous on them with his steam whistle. Mr. Tucker shared of how they, his wartime cavalry found an idle locomotive and tossing a dozen or more ropes on the cab and pull it down during the war, so's to wreck its use. Slim was learning a passel of lessons just for the hearing of it. He never imagined the things these boys knew about fighting for the brand. He was getting the idea of it now. Slim supposed that the railroad would leave "General Tucker" and his cow-troopers alone in the future or pay in blood further.

In the end all was well that ended them days for the boys of the herd. Slim still wondered what was going to commence as he toiled to become a top-notch cowman. He was doubly pleasured to know what was in the li'l citadel and for being alive after goings after that railroad bunch. He enjoyed his brief encounter with his Miss Denise. Slim was proud to know his boss, Mr. (General) Tucker, and the O U T outfit could pull together in a time of calamity to put a whooping of a fight on any adversary. And to answer Slim, and in words Kid so loved to pitched, "Name me a war cowmen ever lost!" He was right by Slim's surmise.

Kid and Slim would soon be healed up following the range war and Kid had discovered a new friend in Slim, as Slim was learning answers for all his query and effort. Slim was in wonderment of the awesome firepower he'd just witnessed, a twelve-pounder Napoleon cannon and two ten barrel Gatlin guns. This was all about a week like he'd never thought might happen where he was. Most important, Slim now knew the sure fire cure for divesting an unwanted railroad. But the world wasn't done challenging Slim and Kid, not just yet.

# Chapter IX

## A BAD DAY AND A GOOD FRIEND

"Pow-pow-pow!" And as the gunfire intensified upon Slim, he grumbled to himself how he hated being away from ranch house for this very reason, being shot at on the job. Slim's grumblings were pretty normal at this point in his new craft. Ornery had cautioned of this peril a time or two. Ornery, in fact, was supposed to be away to town on the boss' bidding. Slim pondered as to how he was going get himself out of this with his hide intact. Now it wasn't that Slim didn't love being a cowman out west; it was just that he didn't want to die out west, at least not just yet.

In his favor, he had his prized shooter, an old battered, tarnished up 1866 First Model Winchester* lever rifle at his side. With that, admittedly, he'd guv up his pony and singled out a derned fine tree spot initially to provide him some cover, at least for the moment. And for the time Slim was pleasured with his guv troubled state of affairs.

He didn't cotton* to or care much for this "high profiled lead-slingin' contest," as Ornery would have called this "fit and fix".

So it was that Slim did his best at saving himself, rifle in hand, against the saddle-mounted cattle thieving vermin. Now what it was was that not very many minutes prior some poaching men just happened on Slim and his collection of hapless collection of beeves that day. Slim's cows, all of which were thoroughly scattered by now, looked to end up in brand new ownership if'n he didn't get busy doing his crafting properly.

Actually, they weren't Slim's beeves, but Mr. Tucker's for sure, maybe? Worse than dying was Slim's fear of what Ornery would say by Slim guvin' into the rustlers and letting them make off with their share of the herd. Ornery would be far harsher on Slim than anything Mr. Tucker would do or say to him, so's he figured. In fact, Slim un-disremembered* Mr. Tucker telling his cowhands, Slim included, that he expected every man, "to carry his own weight and to do what he was hired to do." Though the boss didn't require his cow-saddlers to buck the tiger* when the chips were clearly against them. Mr. Tucker knew that he'd always fetch up more beeves, but experienced and dedicated punchers could be bit harder to come by. Nevertheless, for now, that was of a no-never-mind to Slim for he was a dead man either way, Ornery or not.

Slim's way of things was this, he'd never fire a shot for the heck of it and he'd never guv much thought about killing folk outright, either. However, he knew when he was faced with a game of, "Him or Me", today, well; it was definitely going be "him" not "me", Slim deliberated. The young saddler wasted no time extricating a hand full of rounds off his cartridge belt and swift-ed them in the loading gate of his rifle.

Slim prepared for the next go at those ill gotten and ill gained band of ne'er-do-wells to his front. As Slim had feared, the five remaining rustlers were working their way around his tree trying to box him up. He realized he wasn't going to be able to out maneuver them before they shot him, "two ways from Texas", as Ornery oft' said. In retrospect Slim realized his hiding hole was, at best a poor place, as he observed the outlaws forming a line formation in front of him. There'd been eight rustlers to start. One was shot out of his saddle and another hurting to bad so's not to make any more grief for others in life, as Slim would later confirm. Now it was just a matter of minutes before Slim was done for, dead and gone.

Slim calculated the whereabouts of the two nearest bushwhackers by the clamor they were generating as their hurried their way through the brush, and over the lose rocks on their way to Slim; there was an awkward moment of silence all about him. Hugging the ground tightly, Slim struggled to listen to what was going to happen next.

And, he thought for a split second of how he wished Ornery was near at hand and just about this now.

Suddenly all tar nation busted lose in a frenzied field of gunfire. Slim instantly shifted his prone body to the left side of the tree trunk base, hugging it for cover. He set his sight picture on the first thing that availed itself and fired without hesitation. Slim filled the coming encroaching rustler with two lumps of hot lead, quick up. He rolled himself away from that spot again to get away from the gun smoke so's to fetch a clearer shot at whatever appeared next. Still flat on his belly, as he positioned his rifle sites on the next vertical form that came straight on him, Slim realized his gig was up as he seemingly did his last earthly doing of life that day. For a flash his mind's eye pictured a grieving Miss Denise and how distressed she'd be to learn of his miserable and untimely demise against so many rustlers. And finally, he pondered another swift cogitation about death, and in that moment muttered this laconic plea, "Save me, Lord!"

The rustlers were on the move coming down on him fast, and shooting at him too. There's no way he'd burn 'em all down, take the fight and win the day, alive. Slim wasn't certain for certain where his pony was now either, so's a getaway was well out of the question.

From where the bushwhackers started their charge on him and by the means for which Slim had to make his last stand... well... he was a goner and he knew it. With nothing to lose but his life, Slim just started shooting up a black powder storm. This was Slim's "finest hour," and perhaps his final moments of cowman glory, as he fought his heart out for 'the brand' and his beeves.

These bad boys meant business and for now Slim was their business. There was no going back as Slim aimed down his rifle barrel and made it blow smoke and spit lead. All the while clumps of dirt, shards of lead and slivers of tree bark flew every which direction about him, as the buzzing hunks of hot lead ricocheted off the rocks, the roots and the tree trunk around him.

The gun smoke got so thick Slim couldn't see but only a few long feet around at most. As the smoke enveloped him he heard and felt the gunfire and heavy footsteps closing down on him by the rustlers. By his ears it didn't sound purdy to him at all.

Through all of the commotion Slim strangely detected a change in the tempo of his attackers, as the sounds of folk and metal hitting the ground, like their legs were chopped out from under them was going on. The shooting stopped. He quit up his gunfire but remained at the ready and waited very quietly.

Circumstances were getting beyond Slim's comprehension because he couldn't discern what was commencing around him for the smoke and the silence. So he went back to shooting at the noises to his front. With no warning the hair on the back of Slim's neck stood up. He swiftly rolled on his back, just in time to point his rifle up at a horse-mounted rider at his back. This man just stared him down, a pair of revolvers in his horse-mounted hands.

Slim immediately recognized the horse and its rider from his 'running out of room' hiding place, and said, "Yer a sight fer sore eyes... an' achin' bones!" Slim was sorely pleasured to see this face too. The face staring down on him wasn't Ornery, but another member of the outfit and very good partner to know, the 'Yellowstone Kid', cow detective. At that moment Kid sat erect in the saddle, a taut rope running off his saddle horn and long across the smoke filled path. His pair of Walker-Colt horse revolvers hoisted at the ill-mannered ne'er-do-well boys, or what was left of them.

Now all four whole bandits had parted themselves from their shooters* they'd been packing and got on their feet having been freshly stumbled by Kid's *latigo* string, no worse for the wear, sorta-kinda. With grave regret one of them crossways jaspers still had some play left in him. He swift-like moved to challenge the mounted shootist by filling his hand with a belly gun, a small revolver, and commenced to throw down on Kid.

Not wanting to disappoint the fool-minded sporting man Kid let loose a volley from his pair of hand cannons and cut the *bandito** down, all while covering the same in a field of gun smoke. Slim simultaneously rolled back to his belly and leveled his rifle at the remaining un-stumbled rustlers.

For a long moment all was quiet, save the echo of the last gun blast dispensed by Kid. Also, the moaning of the most recently chest and belly shot *hombre*\*. During that moment Slim recollected all that had come loose around him and took a second to soak it in. He was still pleasured up to see Kid and so very pleasured for having him backing his play against them folly-boys. Slim had guv up and figured himself buzzard bait by now. He'd been done for if'n it hadn't been for Kid, who now always appeared at trouble like a ghost.

"How're ya' doin' Slim?" asked Kid, Slim lying there keeping a sharp eye on those rustlers.

"I've been better," Slim answered. "So where'd ya' come from?"

"Oh, out from headquarters lookin' fer ya'," Kid said, a hinting chuckle in his voice, "and before that, the Yellowstone River Valley, and before that, my Ma!" Slim couldn't cogitate no clever response, so he said, "Well, I'm dern'ed glad I brung ya' then!" Kid laughed and said, "Ya' brin' these hapless hooligans, as well?"

"NO!" Slim retorted, "they was a lookin' fer ya' with their guns out and got me instead. An' then, as it was, I proved to be too much gun fer 'em." Kid let loose good belly laugh and said, "So that's why they was a rushin' on ya' like that, huh?"

"Ya' done did see it fer yer'n own, didn't cha?" Slim proudly queried.

"Well, Mr. Lead Magnetic Personage," Kid said, "Ya'd better git on o'er and finish 'em up, don't ya' think? Oh, and make derned certain ya' bind 'em boys together right tight like now!" As Slim did go to this chore he asked, "Kid, how'd ya' git that sting o' yers out so's to confound the feet o' this bunch?"

"Now, Slim," replied Kid, "if I tolt'cha all how I done my detective craft, ya'd be wanta be a cow detective and I'd be outta a work now, won't I?"

"I reckon'spect* so," Slim answered.

Kid rounded up Slim's Pete, along with the rustler's ponies, and guv Slim some string to use on the tie up the sad jaspers. The two O U T cowmen finished cinching the cattle thieves to their very own animals; Slim thanked Kid genuinely for his assistance upon this little chore. He assured Kid he couldn't have done it without him.

Kid mentioned it was all about his pleasure to be of assistance where he could, for that's what his job as the cow detective was all about. Kid next quizzed Slim to the whereabouts of Ornery. Slim shared that Ornery might well be back up at ol' N̲o̲. 7 from town fixing up the livestock pen and the shack, he sorely hoped anyway.

They took hold of their party of eight, some dead, some not and took them back to the line shack. Ornery was plenty pleasured, surprised and somewhat puzzled to see Slim riding in minus his beeves, but with Kid and some others not so invited and otherwise wrecked.

After an early dinner and a brief visit, Kid expressed he'd be contented to take the "ne'er do wells" back to face the local county sheriff, in Well Springs.

"If'n there's any bounty out fer any o' these critters, I'll fetch it back to ya', Slim."

"Good up and half o' its yers." He was plenty pleasured to be rid of the whole lot of them cow thieves. He said, "Take good care and go good." Ornery just couldn't help himself and reminded Slim, saying, "What he means is the half reward fer savin' his skin!" Slim ignored Ornery asking Kid, "Guv any reward I git comin' to Mrs. Tabishman's… I mean Miss Brennan's school children's offerin'." Kid said he'd be back out their way as soon as he was done in town with them thieves. He also said he'd stop off at the big house to fill Mr. Tucker's ear with the details of how Slim saved the herd and such stuff.

With that, Kid inspected his motley collection before going. Slim called out again, "Go good, Kid!" Ornery hollered, "Don't fergit to go by Vandelhorn's General Store and fetch me back some fresh tobacc'a." Kid nodded to both requests.

So Slim told Ornery about his earlier ordeal with the rustlers. He was curious to why Ornery hadn't come to the gunplay. Ornery assured Slim he never attended any party that he wasn't invited too or knew none about. Slim agreed. He was a grateful cowman, mightily pleasured for a true friend in the person that was the, Yellowstone Kid.

But now the question begged, what if you guv Slim a lot of rope like the one Kid had? Would he hang himself or another? Ornery would find out all too soon.

# Chapter X

## A ROPE AND A LIFE OF BALANCE

Ornery did share that in this cow craft certain dangers filled nearly each and every hour of each and every day. It was for this very reason experienced top hands and cowmen got testy with them 'arbuckles'* of the outfit from time to time. It wasn't that they didn't like the new cowhands, but to fetch a fresh cowman's focus and keep him on this side of the sod, alive, was nigh on a full time job just behind working the herd. Getting betwixt and between a cow and a greener made that toil some dangerous for even the best top hand cowmen. And this then was the predicament facing Ornery with Slim.

What oft' appeared as a callous prank was a gaming way of learning a greener a lesson by the old hands. It was a rare cowman that hadn't suffered nearly every trial that could befall a buckaroo in this craft and Ornery had his tales to tell. So it came as no surprise to even the stoutest, most saddle rode, cowhand to find himself dallied* up in a fit and a fix every once in awhile. Three things seemed to offer paid success to a cowman who abided in these measures.

First, a fine working horse was a must so's to balance the workload and save a fellow from walking. The thought of the word, 'walk', commenced to making a cowman's feet ache mightily just for the mention, a definite four-letter swear word if'n you ever heard one.

Second, was a loyal and knowledgeable saddle partner, as he was a lifesaver from nearly any trouble that faced his partner along any trail ridden, a "buddy system" if you will.

Third, to round out a prairie saddler's gear, he'd need to commence to own a well made, well fitting saddle, lasso-rope, a revolver, and to make proper use of them all. With these things at his side he was a hard one for failing. However, nothing said he'd not 'have his hole', or be buried, in a flash for the lack of good sense and the proper manner of commencing the use of that same.

With all of that said, who was it here that was the better saddler? Was it the old trusty top hand of the outfit, or the good natured, well-intentioned, better lead greenhorn? Life's lessons oft' suggested a balance of; knowledge, skill, wisdom, and personality type which might well demonstrate, in more ways than one, what it took to stay on this side of the sod.

Slim had best recollected that morning so's to Ornery's having had a bad night in his bunk. That merely meant Ornery was gonna be 'heck-on-the-hoof'* the rest of the day, which was all day in this case. Already that morning Ornery had banged about the shack like he had lead in his trouser pockets and his head was out in a pasture else place. Yet things had gone fairly well until the pair set to throw up in their saddles and head out to gather some beeves for Cap'n Stewart later on that day.

As Ornery inspected Slim's horse, saddle cinch, rig and all, things were peaceable. Well, peaceable until Ornery come upon Slim's throwing string, his *latigo* lasso and he shouted, "SLIM! What the world ya' doin' with that long string? There's a 'nuf rope there to hang our whole herd without another rope involved!" Slim shrugging turned away without a word and headed for the shack to pluck down his short string from the wall behind his bunk. Ornery said, "Leave it go an' let's us git to goin' fer we're burnin' daylight foolin' about here." Both cowmen made their saddles, turned their ponies to ride down to the creek to fetch those afore mentioned critters.

As they rode the trail, Slim gawked about the heavens pleasured by the fact it was sunny and not raining like the day before.

"Wha'cha huntin' fer Slim?" asked Ornery. Slim glanced his bunkie and wondered if'n he was in line for harsher reproof from the senior saddler. He pondered his words with great care before speaking, said, "Nut in'. So why's it ya' didn't want me bringin' my long rope today?" Ornery answered, "Slim, weez plenty to do today and ya' ain't the goodest with yer short rope. The long rope is just that much more handicap upon yer throwin' arm and we ain't got time fer it today. Besides, ya' git ta work closer to 'em beeves and that's good fer ya'. Ya' seein' my point?"

"Yep, I do now. So why'd ya' let be brin' it?" Ornery chuckled, saying, "Ya'll ne'er learn that strin' if'n it's hangin' on the wall in the shack!" Eyeing Ornery with curiosity, Slim's eyebrow's raised; he shook his head in amazed concurrence with his senior pard. That made good thinking too, though it seemed some contradictory, them two reasons back to back or so he figured. First it was he wasn't ready for that long rope and suddenly he was. So what was it?

Then Ornery said, "Just one more thin', ya' might desire to rotate yer cartridge belt about yer middle so's not to rub yer cartridges out on the back o' yer high cantle." Slim cranked his head around and run his left hand along his belt only to find nearly every cartridge in the back was worked loose and nearly gone free. Slim replied, "Thank yee!" He thought ol' Ornery might be ornery, but he don't miss a 'stitch', do he? Ornery asked, "Don't that belt bucket eat on yer belly the way ya' got it on ya' like that?" It did but Slim didn't want to fess up he hadn't figured out the easy fix, just yet. They halted while Slim made fix of his cartridge belt and got ready to ride on. They put off again to perform their craft while daylight still favored them.

The two was a busy finding beeves a pair or so at a time as they pushed them to a holding pen down on the big meadow floor southwest of the shack. The morning was plenty warm, a light breeze kept the hard sweat off of them as they worked their doggies*. They worked like a finely oiled machine in and around about the meadow, gathering half the beeves requested by high noon. Ornery called out, "Slim, let's brin' that pair down from the hillside, up by the cut, there." Slim nodded and went high to push them grass grazers down into Ornery's able care.

When Ornery saw the two steers had no intention of crossing the swollen creek, he fetched his *lasso* off his saddle horn and trotted off to have his attention with them. The cow path along the south side of the creek was still very damp, slick and soft from the very recent rains. Ornery stepped his *cabello* up onto the grass covered ledge, just above the path and went swiftly to them.

As Ornery rode toward his catch he spotted a deadfall tree on the path and stepped his mount back down on the trail to put it past him. As he settled his ride back on the muddy cow trail and beyond the obstacle, the trail crumbled in mass out from under him, and his sure-footed saddle-mount. When the ground broke open Ornery and his horse headed on a hard leaning over toward the water swollen quick flowing creek. Ornery stood up hard on his left stirrup, leaning south to shift his balance away from the tipping over side. Slim immediately eyed his pard and from his perspective things looked plum ugly. In an all out dead rush Slim come down off the hill and quick up.

Ornery's situation grew more precarious by the split moment as the ground continued to crumble out under him. Suddenly he and his pony slipped off the crumbling bank side and were swallowed up in the creek. From an overload upon an extreme angle guv it, Ornery's left stirrup strap stripped clean off his saddle. And with that, all of Ornery tipped completely backward and he was put off in the creek with a big splash.

Slim knew peril when he glimpsed it and Ornery was having himself a whole heaping water trough full of peril just this now. He knew he'd dare not go near the creek bank to fetch Ornery and suffer the same calamity. Yet, he knew he'd no time to lose if he was gonna affect a swift recovery of his pard from the swift going creek.

Without thought, Slim swiped his long lasso up and shook out a full size loop and swung it tall. He got a steady bead on Ornery's bobbing head, his rolling trunk, as the water pulled, worked and tugged at the water-logged cowman, his; hat, vest, chaps, boots and all. Slim, out of time, swung his big loop over his head and loosed it with a mighty Houlihan (Hoolihan or Hooly-ann) throw. The coils rapidly reeled from him as Slim's loop sailed out and hit the bobbing Ornery squarely. Slim cut his horse about and headed back toward the hillside. He dallied his rope about his saddle horn on the fly and gentled up on his rope as he drew out the slack and his partner as he wrangled Ornery out of the creek and up over the bank to the grassy meadow floor.

With Ornery on dry ground Slim stopped his forward motion and backed up his pony to slack his rope and loosed it off his saddle horn, so's not to drag Ornery any further. In a hurry Slim kicked down off his horse and went back down his string to where Ornery lay on the ground. Ornery lay motionlessly, but still sucking wind, barely.

"How ya' feelin', Ornery? Can I get' cha anythin'?" After a bit, words.

"No, especially nothin' with water in it!" Slim caught the big man's sarcastic tone and dropped to the grass laughing uncontrollably. He knew his pard was, well, wet and no worse for the wear. Now both laughed until they were nigh on to tears for the pain of that laughter.

When Ornery got his wind, for the second time in the past few minutes, he said, "Don't ya' e'er let me tell ya', ya' cain't throw yer rope, my friend!"

"I'll hol' ya' to that one," Slim replied, smiling. He got up and assisted Ornery back onto his wet water soggy boots. Ornery shook off Slim's loop, they shook hands, and they parted for their respective ponies.

Ornery's Blackie regained his footing and was back on the grass once the ill-balanced rider was loosed off him. By in by the beast appeared to be in good order, munching grass, while Ornery's saddle was in much need of a new stirrup, stirrup leather and fixing. Ornery limped along, his wrecked riding rig over to the corral. Slim took his Pete; his long rope, and fetched home the two steers that had brought on this forlorn calamity.

Later, Slim rode to the corral and was greeted by Cap'n Stewart, Wyatt, Hap, and Ornery. Slim swung down from his horse and shook the hands of his co-workers.

"What's this I hear o' a wreck yer partner done up?" Cap'n asked Slim.

"Well, I reckon I didn't fetch Ornery's canteen full enough water, so's he got this powerful thirst that only that th'ar creek could supply and now here he is, Cap'n," Slim said, a big smile on his face. Remarks of a similar nature followed on by the rest of the party from Slim's words.

"True...true, like a month's wages, I had it comin' to me," said Ornery, in jest, "I was dispensin' heavy grief earlier today and I deserve yer "kindness" in return. I guv Slim pure guff about his long rope and his not bein' no good at throwin' it, so's to save his soul, then he shows me, by savin' mine." Again they kindly ribbed Ornery for being... well, as usual, ornery!

As Cap'n Stewart and party prepared off for the home place, he said he'd have Hap bring Ornery a second saddle during his rounds. They'd fetch his broken one back home for mending. The three ranch riders headed the cows back while Ornery and Slim looked on them for a time. Then they too made ready to ride back up to the line shack.

"Slim," Ornery said, "ya' done me proud today with yer rope, I won't fergit cha fer it neither. I know I git kinda mean at ya' some. However, ya've learnt good by me; yer ridin', cuttin' and ropin' skills, and ya' done us plum proud today, thanks!" Slim smiled shyly and said, "The thanks is all mine fer the saddler ya've made me, and besides Ornery, we're loyal pards, remember? So can I go to town and visit with Miss Denise fer a time?" Ornery chuckled at Slim's query, "Don'cha go gittin' *loco* on me now, my LOYAL pard." Both took a look around and rode on to the shack, being done for the day. Slim reckoned it queer his seeing Ornery riding bareback on his pony like he done it every day and all the time.

So that's how it played out that day on Sorry Dog Creek of the O U T Spread. The balance in life that day had been a good and long rope, a dependable and steadfast partner and swell learning, keeper of them three afore mentioned cow codes. Ornery and Slim both learned that a well lead arbuckle could save the day of the best-est top hand, all while working the herd in full truth of the matter. Ornery began to think that maybe Slim wasn't really all that green any more. However, what they couldn't see approaching was an unexpected pair of riders, on another day, one of them female, coming by a point and time to their very corner of the spread.  What did this mean and would it bring

deathly peril or fortuitous blessing?

# Chapter XI

## THE SCHOOLMARM'S SUMMER VISIT TO OL' No. 7

Ornery and Slim nodded to the Yellowstone Kid as they watched him ride away. Kid reciprocated as he rode out. Kid was headed for Well Springs, as they were headed nor' west up Big Wind Canyon, around Splendid Valley Overhang to ol' No. 7 line shack. It was just first light as the three riders took to going off the yard of the O U T Spread headquarters, a day full of bizarre happenstance awaiting them.

As Kid arrived to town it was the eighth hour according to his vest pouch chronometer*. He took to looking about for the attractively clad, eye-pleasing, and most popular lady of learning, schoolmarm, Miss Lisa Brennan. He soon discovered she wasn't to be found at the schoolhouse, the library, the church or her boarding house at the Ellington Place. Not until Kid spake to Miss Ellington at the doctor's office did he learn that Miss Brennan was gone off on her way to the Twenty Spread, '*Dos XX's*' by the local boys and *vaqueros** to visit.

Miss Denise said, "I don't know when Lisa left town this morning, but she's going out to the Double X to give reading and writing lessons to cowhands. Lisa will be back in town tomorrow, she hoped, anyway." Kid thanked her and went on his way.

Next he went to Mr. Grimm's Gun Emporium, on East Front Street, just a few doors down from the Doc's to fetch new gun parts and fresh cartridges for his rifle and newest revolver. Kid left the emporium and thought he ought go to the Twenty Spread to guv Rafe Johnson, his cow detective counter part, a 'howdy', and perhaps, escort Miss Brennan back safely to town. Kid fetched his horse from livery and a few supplies from the General Store before going on out of town to find her.

Meanwhile, Miss Brennan rode for her far off destination. She'd made her preparation the night before and was gone to the Twenty Spread before daybreak. She rode on her treasured Pinto* guv her by Mr. Tucker. As it wasn't the time of year when children were in school, so Miss Brennan earned much of her keep in the summer tutoring, teaching, and offering instruction to the local cowboys and older folk in her community.

For her great worldly knowledge and selfless service she was highly regarded; a favored and sought after soul, enjoyed for her company as much as for her edifying of folks and children alike. The schoolmarm was spanking brand new to town earlier that spring so's to replace the ailing and weary, Mrs. Tabishman, an equally pleasant older lady. Miss Brennan, her surname of Ireland, guv by the import(*ance*); 'teardrop, sadness or sorrow', was genuinely well-breed, well-mannered, and well-educated gal, a much refined young lass. She was exceptionally polite, easy-going, exceedingly pious and sincerely so, a Sabbath keeper. She was a peaceable sort unless compelled against her pleasant will, then she was bold and formidable in defense her students, her friends or herself. Within her lay an extraordinarily adventurous personage, one that well explicated her having been out in the midst of the untamed frontier west.

Equally intriguing was her wardrobe that showcased her frontier spirit exceedingly swell. It was refined, smartly crafted, and tailor made of the finest quality materials of the latest fashion of those found in San Francisco, New York, and the Parisian persuasion. On that day, thanks to her newly made and kindred lady-friends, she was clad in a functionally elegant outfit that shielded her from chin to toe, head to foot, as she rode the hills and prairie. Miss Lisa wore frontier clothing assembled by Miss Shannon Emory the local professional seamstress with assistance from Miss Ellington.

Her ensemble featured a short tan flat topped crown on a large flat brimmed hat, for plenty of shade, with a stampede string*, a matching tan blouse-skirt set, and a chocolate brown waist sash. Her blouse, a stout woven cotton with long sleeves, reinforced cuffs, and fully white silk lining, and sported a tall straight neck collar for protection from the elements. About her diminutive waist was a skirt kin to that of a Wyoming Riding* style, with a pair of flap covered front pockets. The skirt went all the way down to her ankles; ankles clad securely by her nearly knee high leather lace up boots. Completing her garb was a pair of gauntlet style riding gloves and a serape (sari-rah'-pay), to boot. Her apparel covered her loveliness in whole, all but her button purdy face. The schoolteacher looked like a *gaucho*-gal, or a lady-*vaquero* (or *vaquera**). She was a charm to behold in all her riding finery.

Her pinto was mated up to her very own fine Cheyenne roll saddle, saddlebags full up with a day's provisions, water canteen, small primer bag and reticule secured to her rig and saddle horn, respectively. All of this as her rode onto the Twenty Spread cutting across a piece of the O U T's northwest corner country.

All morning Miss Brennan rode the wide open and rolling prairie with nary a soul to be seen unto her own. Nonetheless, she began to sense that perhaps someone or something was nigh at hand. She went along a primitive trail not far from a tree line and the stream. Sudden like, without warning she was struck in the back of her head, just under her hat, on her hair clasp by an object that had come from the nearby scrubby line of tall brush at her back. Though the object was clearly a crudely fashioned arrow, as she'd later discover, it might have injured her just the same if'n it had struck her much harder.

The arrow struck Miss Brennan snapping in half her bow shaped hair clasp. As she was struck she reflexively snatched her hand back to her hair bun and clasp only being able to fetch back the rod portion of that hair clasp. As the arrow and broken clasp pieces fell to the ground behind her and her horse, she instinctively twisted her head left, then right, to glimpse if'n she might the spot where or who'd sent the arrow at her back. From an intuitive sense of caution she swiftly coaxed her pony into a canter going for the tree line and the stream to depart from her would be attacker, or attackers.

Once inside the meager tree line, Miss Brennan took stock in her situation, location, and to see if'n a soul or more were in pursuance of her. When Miss Lisa saw she was relatively relieved from harm's way, she made certain that her saddle rig and gear was intact, and it was. She paused to offer a brief prayer of thanks for receiving no real injury.

As Ornery and Slim rode for No. 7, Slim was curious so he asked Ornery, "How many outfits have cow detectives like Kid?" Ornery answered, "Well, Iz cain't say fer certain, but many ranches sufferin' rustlin' do thar best to git a hired gun to save thar herds."

"So who's the best detective of 'em all, Ornery?"

"Shame be on ya' Slim! Why it's the Yellowstone Kid, o' course." Ornery had no real idea who that really was, yet figured this was crackerjack answer enough for Slim.

All the while, Miss Brennan continued riding nearer to the stream and soon emerged from the trees and straight away made notice of a lean looking she-cat mountain lion staring her down. With most hasty dispatch the schoolteacher fetched her small Colt "Baby Dragoon" pocket revolver from her little handbag cinched at the saddle horn. As the big cat bore down upon Miss Brennan and her pinto, she discharged her first shot. The small thirty-one-caliber revolver ball raced out scuffing off the dirt causing the cat to swerve swiftly to the left. In a quick successive motion the 'marm loosed away two more shots from her 3-1/2 inch barreled five-shot percussion revolver, all while her pinto danced about wildly.

In the fracas of this charging cat, revolver smoke, fire and lead on dancing pony, Miss Brennan managed to dissuade the she mountain lion away from her, at which time she too took to galloping away. She rode quickly up along across the streambed where she didn't slow down until she rounded the spot that deposited her at the Splendid Valley Overhang.

Once up under the overhang she took note of three things with her arrival. First, just how splendid the view was from where she was sat. Second, her pinto was favoring its rear left leg, a stone bruise, perhaps from her mad get-a-way at the streambed. And finally, she noted her primer bag had gotten loosed up and departed from her, probably during the kitty-cat fracas, back up the trail.

Distraught for the loss of her basic trade tools and in want of needed assistance on the moment, because of her lamed pony, she was beside herself. The teacher dismounted taking off her saddlebags and small hand purse. On the ground she commenced to inspect her horse and as she suspected, it was a mild stone bruise of the tendon, the deep flexor tendon. Still sensing someone was close by; she stayed closer by her horse, her hand Bible, her handbag, and hand shooter. She knelt to the ground, relaxing herself by deep breathing and mediation.

The young lady offered herself in prayer, pleading for guidance, wisdom and safe recovery of her misplaced property. She quietly prayed David's Ninety-First Psalm, one of her and her papa's favorite bible passages. Miss Brennan was mentally and physically buried in mediation when she was startled to reality by a familiar voice.

"Howdy Miss Brennan," Kid called out as he rode to where she was knelt inside the overhang.

"How do you do, good sir?"

"Am I a interferin' upon ya' here?"

"No, not anymore, Kid, and what brings you out here on a fine summer day?"

"Honestly? A well deserved visit to Twenty Spread, and ya', actually." Then Kid held out her wayward tote, a bit roady, or dirty, from his saddle made lap for all the world to see. Kid inquired, "What may I ask has ya' out this here on such a fine summer day?" The marm answered, "Same as you, I reckon." Kid couldn't resist her choice of words and said, "So, same as me, huh? Does that mean ya' was out here to visit the Double X and, me?" She smiled at him and very politely posed her next question, ignoring his query, the 'me' part and said, "How's your head doing?" He guv her a queer glance, replying, "I'm a' sane a man as the next I reckon, why?" She contained her laughter with a broad smile and said, "No, I mean how is that head wound of your? The one you had the first time we met?" Kid cogitated upon her words; an image of her came to mind.

It was the image of the first time he'd laid eyes on her. He recollected the schoolmarm looked more like a field hospital nurse than a teacher that day. Her sleeve cuffed back a couple of turns exposing her delicate hands, wrists, and forearms. Her brunette hair was ruffled from its drawn bun and a sprig of it hanging in her face apiece. She'd a smudge of dried blood on the tip of her dainty nose and right cheek and wearing a darling smile. That's how Kid first recollected her, a portrait of beauty and manners for all to behold.

Now Kid had to contain his laughter as he un-disremembering* his manners and kicked off his horse. He fetched her book tote to her directly. Kid replied, "I'm feelin' capital and its nice o' ya' to ask." Again, he wasn't able to resist the moment, asking, "Miss Brennan, if'n yer headed fer the Double X, why 'er ya' here on 'this' spot o' Mister Tucker's O U T Spread and a fair ways from yer course?" She replied,

"Oh dear, Kid, am I that way far from my original destination? I was so ready to be at the Double X by now. Will Mister Tucker be disconcerted with me for my inadvertent trespassing upon his property?"

Kid smiled broadly, "Only if'n he finds ya' hurt or dead, fer he, like plenty folk 'round here are plenty pleasured up to have ya' 'round these parts. I'm certain ya' 'er welcome on the spread anytime ya' please, okay?" She nodded at Kid guvin' him a pleasant smile of relief.

Miss Brennan told how an arrow came from behind, striking her head mounted hair clasp, breaking it. Then of her going through the tree line to get away from her attacker, then about the mountain lion and now her lame pony. Kid agreed she was having a crackerjack of a day already and it wasn't yet noonday. He assured her it was a good thing that he'd happened along when he did. Kid produced two pieces that made up her hair cinch, as he called it. She retained the shaft piece and pulled it from her handbag. Based on the evidence Kid had guv up, Miss Brennan began to wonder if'n he'd been trailing her all the way from headquarters, or perhaps even town? Yet, she reckoned he was with her and that said he'd found her going his way somehow.

Kid told her about a pair of school-aged boys that had been near the stream a ways back and may have been the likely culprits of her arrow attack, being he'd seen them in the possession of a very crudely fashioned bow. Next he referenced to her about some long grooved, small caliber dirt scuffs on the ground and a light blood trail he'd seen on his ride back about a place she spake of earlier.

She went on to tell and he listened to her story intently. Kid asked, "Did ya' shoot yer shooter dry… er empty I mean?" She shook her head and produced her small Colt revolving cylinder pocket pistol for his sufficient inspection. In his mind Kid thought mighty highly of a calico who toted her very own shooter.

"May I assist ya' in a more proficient and harmonious outcome with yer pistol purse piece?" Kid queried her. She flashed a polite smile at him, pondering his words.

"Yes, but will it take much time?" Kid returned her smile with one of his own and answered, "Well, that will very much depend upon ya'. I mean no offense."

"None taken," she said, "Oh, and if you will permit me to return the favor in assisting you with some reading lessons, okay?" Kid let go a hearty laugh, replying, "Ya' gotta deal there, ma'am!"

The schoolmarm changed the topic before he could renege on their deal, as he called it. She asked, "Would you like a blueberry muffin and some warm tea to drink?" Kid replied, "Why certainly and let me see if'n I can git the fire pit over there sparked back to life. Then we'll boil us up some water fer tea." Discovering small embers, coals still burning in the fresh ash, Kid produced a short, eight-inch, copper blowpipe from the bottom of his saddlebags. He fetched some tinder of pine twigs and wood chips along with some prairie coal* from a pile not far from the pit.

Soon Kid had a flame going, burning enough to light up the dried cow chips in the pit. Miss Brennan voiced her curiosity to whom or what might have been there so recent so's to leave fresh coals in the fire pit and fuel for the fire? Kid calmed her worries by suggesting that it was just Ornery and Slim as they made their way out to their O U T line shack that morning. His explanation satisfied her and this put her mind at ease.

Miss Brennan set about cleaning up the dirty kettle left there by very thoughtful souls. Kid fetched back his water canteen and soon she'd water on to slow boil. She fetched a small tea tin; drink cups and a pair of partly mashed muffins from her saddlebags.

As they sat patiently waiting for the water to boil, she queried, "Who are you, Kid and what are really called?" Looking her straight on he flashed an unassuming half-smile, but remained silent, not offering her any reply. The look on his face as he pondered her question, suggested to her a glimpse of great internal pain with him. The kind of pain that said he couldn't begin to share his story with one as lovely as herself, at least not immediately.

So she began explicating herself to him to break the ice, socially. Soon Kid was all about her every word. Miss Brennan was from somewhere near a place named, Vancouver, in the Washington Territory, being one of the diminutive few folk having come 'east' to abode in the cattlemen's west. She was the middle child of three daughters from a family ostensibly well set, via logging and mining wealth. Unlike Miss Ellington, Miss Brennan hadn't been schooled in the east exclusively, though she'd received some schooling in Charleston, in the south of the Carolinas. Miss Lisa had traveled for years with her papa to London, Paris, Madrid, Berlin, and Rome of Europe. She'd journeyed to; Athens of Greece, Jerusalem, Beirut, Damascus of Palestine, Cairo and Alexandria of Egypt, schooling in international settings in a worldly manner.

It was then her head yearned to learn at every chance guv her and it was there in her young life her heart was called, so preciously, to education. She desired to teach others, mainly children and child-like minds, wherever she traveled. Minds like the one she had witnessed in Kid and other cowhands in her brand-new community, her new home, as they were fertile soil for learning.

Miss Lisa explained; for all her travel, it was the long absences from home, where she missed her mama that sometimes troubled her so. She was close to her mama, but fonder just a tiny bit more of her papa. As for her sisters, "they were more like bosom chums, dear friends, and so they were," she said. The teacher was christened, Lisa Annette Brennan, by her papa and mama. She oft' was fondly referred to by her siblings as, 'Lisa-Anne' or simply, 'Annie'. Miss Lisa spoke lovingly of her family, yet, she seemed somehow removed from them, both emotionally and very physically there now in Wyoming.

She spake to her love for the Lord, for her family upbringing that had her so much brought her to that love. Kid listened fixed, filled with a grand fascination of her every story within her stories, as the tea was ready and she served it. He reckoned that as fulfilled as she was, flush with all her fresh successes in her present situation, she appeared to have a 'hole' inside her. A big hole in her heart, no less, or so's he pondered.

Kid wasn't a total cowman, nonetheless, he was plenty familiar with the craft to a great measure, and believed her 'hole' was for the herding instinct, or family desire, perhaps, just a man of her own and some children too. That's the way he read her words. After all, he was a gunman and an able minded gunman had to be clever enough to read folk in order to stay on this side of the sod. She was awful 'brennan' by old Isles standards so's he reckoned.

Miss Brennan's story touched a nerve in Kid causing him to swiftly un-disremember his former life and those earlier days of old. That said, Kid found himself a bit unnerved, as he fiddled about with a short stick in the midst of the coals of the fire pit some, as they partook of cake and drink, and chitchatted.

Suddenly he just blurted it out, forcefully, nearly startling the young teacher from her wits, "Karl Isaiah Dortmund," he said, "My name's Karl Dortmund!" The young woman sat a mite stunned and pondering his bold and boisterous verbiage for a second, and said, "So you come by the name 'Kid', because of your name's set of initials?" Miss Brennan surmised, "How clever."

Then Kid told of his being a half-breed, not fit the company of folk as fine as she, whatever that was supposed to mean. That was his assumption, not hers, or her feelings on this topic whatsoever. Kid told how his mother was Arikara Indian and his father, a German-Irish immigrant tinker. Karl had been born at turn out time, springtime that was, near the confluence of Powder River and the Yellowstone River, in the Montana Territory. However, he spent most of his growing up time along the banks of the Yellowstone River from Lake Yellowstone to near the home of the Mandan tribe in the Dakota Territory, hunting, trapping, and trading for a living.

He shared of a time, as a young trooper scout, when he, for Colonel Custer of the US Seventh Cavalry back in '74 (1874), went with the Black Hills Expedition. There he got the name, 'Kid' by Colonel Custer's Seventh Cavalry Paymaster, 'cuz first, he was a kid back then. Second, Kid only knew how to scribe his initials, "K-I-D". When he drew his monthly roll from the Paymaster or receive government issued equipment from the Quartermaster, he'd scribe his mark with, "K" "I" "D". And, later the Colonel was confounded by who was who, by names, his Aide-de-Camp hung the handle, 'Yellowstone' on 'Kid', and henceforth, Karl became the, "Yellowstone Kid."

Meanwhile, Miss Lisa exacted her well-practiced listening skills and was all ears, taking in ever word Kid shared. Hearing this, she queried, "What's your Arikara family name?" He sat a moment deliberating her question and a fitting answer. Stone-faced he spake, "I'm called, '*One-Who-Dreams-of-Her*', by my people, and '*Warrior-without-Shadow*", by the Crow and Lakota. Only ever did my pa and a man named, Elder White, ever call me, Karl." Again Miss Lisa asked, "Why by those names?" Kid answered, "Partly cuz my mother said, 'my eyes was lookin' fer some special someone,' or my mother's mother said, 'Because he looks for his mother.' As for the tribes, they did so for the manner in which I hunted down and 'venged on the Crow and Sioux warriors that had stolen and later killed my mother. I done this without bein' found out, until to late, and in the light of day no less, unto my enemies. My pa got kill't fightin' 'em, the Crows fer the killin' o' my ma and for his stolen horses. Pa fought bravely and died with honor, they both did. I fought 'em too, but they hit me on the bean and left me fer dead, but I was eight-years-old back then."

The pair sat quite still and quiet for nigh on five minutes, as they finished their warm tea. Miss Lisa carefully pondered his words feeling Kid was still in anguish, anger and remorse over all of this. She eyed him and it was painfully obvious to her that for all of the killings, deaths inflicted in revenge for his ma and pa that he'd gained not one single ounce of personal pride, relief or satisfaction for having done so.

Miss Brennan also observed how Kid hadn't told his story oft' or visited these words with others, if'n ever. Kid looked up, gazing into her face requesting, "Please ne'er repeat this...this what I tol't ya' ta another soul, please! Also, ne'er, ne'er speak the name 'Karl' to me or another soul either. Just e'er only call me, Kid." He finally interjected, "Moreover, thank ya' so kindly fer sharin' yer story with me and permittin' me to say mind."

It was agonizingly clear to the marm as to why this man was what the cowmen called a, 'Mavericker', a man not socially well blended, a loner, and a man unto his own. His story explained to her best why he, a professional cow detective, or hired gun, was the personage he was or had become. She smiled, scooted over toward him and took his right hand gently in hers. She finally replied, "No, thank you for hearing me out and for sharing your awesomely powerful personal story." She continued, "I reckon today was our time we were purposed to share such things, together. I'll not repeat your story or your 'Karl' name to no one. Also, I'd be pleasured...is that how you men say that? I'd be pleasured if you'd please call me, 'Lisa' from now on." Kid squeezed her hand gently and teasingly of course said, "Ya' sure drive a hard bargain, Miss Brennan, but I believe I can honor that request o' yers... Lisa!"

They laughed as they sat their cups on the ground and rose to their feet to walk to the horses.

"I believe I owe ya' a shootin' lesson today?"

"I may regret this, yet I believe you do."

"Nice 'John B' ya've got on yer head, Miss Lisa," said Kid. "Ya' might wish to stow yer hat and poncho before we git goin' here." She went to her saddle and stowed her poncho and hat by the stampede string to the saddle horn. She fetched back her shooter and reloading pouch. Her *pistolero* set off to fetch gear out of his bags on his horse.

After Kid hobbled their ponies he helped look after Miss Lisa as they took their belongings and moseyed down to the front of the overhang. Kid set a half dozen old rusted up and battered holed up cups and cans from the fire pit. In a business like manner he commenced to edify Miss Lisa upon the manner of proper pistol play.

Kid quizzed the marm of what manner of 'shooter' familiarity she already possessed, and following them words; he showed her how to discern her dominant eye. He did so by having her stand upright, feet at shoulder width and her arms fully extended before her, at eye level, both hands cupped so's to form a bit of a 'diamond' shaped opening in them.

Next he instructed her to peer through the cupped opening in her hands, at a lone Ponderosa pine tree out to her front fifteen yards away. Once she'd done so, he instructed her to slowly retract her arms back toward her face, all while carefully keeping her eyes focused on the pine tree. As she did this, her cupped hands settled over her right eye.

"Good, very good," Kid said. She smiled at him, patiently waiting his next words of instruction. He spake to and demonstrated for her how to stand fittingly for shooting. After Miss Lisa learned to address, or grip, and draw her short shooter, Kid talked her through the aim and to point her shooter, and how the two methods, aiming and pointing, worked for their specific purposes. They practiced aiming some and then pointing for a time, her demure revolver being best for pointing for best results.

Kid was surprised and pleasured with the ease and speed by which his pupil exhibited her fresh skills. They played; cock, point, trigger pull, and her recovery (follow-through) and, again with greater rapidity and precision did his student perform. Once again he was impressed with the lady-pupil's sincere interest, her attention, and her talent to imitate his performance. He talked gunplay; she practiced gunplay until they'd nothing left to share but shoot.

Kid, his back to the set of tin targets, as he faced Miss Lisa, abruptly wheeled about, to his right, ninety degrees, without a word. He drew his holstered hip hung Colt revolver as he went; pointed, cocked, fired, and holstered it in the blink of an eyelash. Miss Lisa mused at all of the smoke, flame, noise and the mere swiftness of his hand. What caught her attention was the tin can that reeled into the air.

"Follow this one!" and he repeated his last play, except now he fired two shots in rapid succession. Again, the object that caught and held her attention was the prancing and dancing tin can. He'd caused a second can to pitch up off the ground and into the air. As the can rose airborne, he struck it a second time with his second shot causing it to whirl about and bounce off the table rock floor. Kid holstered his shooter, quick up, too swift for her eye to keep an eye on. Miss Brennan applauded his sure shooting as she watched the smoke drifted off into the gentle mid-day breeze, and the dust to settle.

Kid turned to her and said, "It's yer turn now!" He saw her smile as she answered, "I'm ready, if you are?" Yet, inside she was wondering if'n she'd do what she'd been shown. This was her moment of truth and she well knew she'd do it, that is, with the aid of her teacher, Kid. He emptied out the spent cartridge cases from his 'Open Top' Colt revolver, Miss Lisa found her spot to stand in front of the row of cans. Then they settle to do some serious shooting.

Kid's pupil started strong with her proper stance, clean draw from her sash-made holster, and a well-executed shot. Her first shot, point of aim went a bit high from her line of targets. With some minor coaching from Kid, Miss Lisa was a sure shot in short shooting. Both being thrilled at her swift shooting success, Kid suspected she wasn't as new to shooting as she let on, and he figured he could learn to live with a calico that could handle her way around a 'shooter'.

Across the valley a pair of cow-saddlers took fair notice of the gunfire commencing on their boss's land. It came from where they'd been earlier that day.

"Sounds like a problem goin' on o'er at the overhang," said Slim with concern.

"If'n I didn't know better," replied Ornery, "I'd think it was the Yellowstone Kid and his shooters gittin' in some target practice or doin' his trade on bad jaspers."

"But he's in town visitin' the new 'marm and the sheriff, or both," replied Slim.

"Let's head o'er and check out all the commotion," Ornery said, "just in case it's ne'er-do-well boys up to mischief on the Tucker Spread." The boys turned their ponies at the commotion and cut a trail to the overhang. And, as they headed that way, Slim wasn't pleasured with the prospect of getting in a running gun-duel with another dangerous band of bad men.

The two "ne'er-do-well gun-duelin' encroachers", meaning Miss Lisa and Kid, back at the overhang were finished with their successful shooting lesson and now it was time for Kid to be the obedient pupil and take his first 'Miss Lisa' reading lesson.

After thirty minutes of primer study they stopped to guv Kid a take a brain break from the book. They stood up and Miss Lisa straightened her skirt and blouse, as Kid dusted off the backside of his britches. In the process of standing and straightening herself Miss Lisa hand lose-d, dropped, her primer. Both made a mad mêlée attempt to retrieve her book in mid flight. For their effort they became entangled one to the other and toppled over to the ground. Forgetting the book, Kid grabbed to catch Miss Lisa so's to break her fall. Struggling to reach out to catch her, he landed flat, under her, landing flat on his back. Miss Lisa landed squarely on her reading pupil, waist-to-waist and face-to-face. In a totally unexpected moment they came together, impacted, face-to-face and lips on lips.

In a flash, their bodies and lips together, it seemed so right, then not. Each recoiled from each other. And suddenly they started laughing, they laughed until they were all in tears from their laughter. Kid slowly sat up and pulled the primer out from under his aching backside and handed it to her. They laughed some more as she sat there now in his lap, chuckling over their embarrassing topple-over incident.

Kid spotted a pair of horse riders coming up toward them. He pushed up his knees to aid Miss Brennan in getting to her feet from his lap. Then he rose up off the rock floor there under the overhang.

"Howdy to camp," Ornery shouted, smelling the smoke of the fire and spying the pair inside the overhang.

"Same to ya', Ornery," Kid called back.

"Er weez interruptin' somethin'?" Ornery inquired.

"No," Miss Brennan hurriedly replied, "we're done reading for now, Mr. Ornery."

No sooner had she spake those words and Kid looked at Ornery and to Slim.

Slim, already wearing a big smile turned his face away to conceal that smile for he knew what was about to commence, having seen this before. At that instant Ornery started on Miss Brennan with his pseudo diatribe.

"Ma'am," he retorted, "ya' may address me as, 'Mr. O'Connor' or 'Mr. Patrick' or 'Pat' or just plain ol' 'Ornery'. But ne'er, e'er call me 'Mr. Ornery', fer it somehow implies that I'z the top win-ni-nest recipient o' some fool-hearty contest fer bein' the most, best-est 'ornery' yahoo or some such thin' like that!"

Miss Brennan stood there; her head lowered wearing a slight smile. Ornery could no longer contain himself and busted out uproarious laughter as he swung down from his saddle and approached Miss Brennan and Kid. Ornery reached out and shook Kid's hand, and tipped his hat to Miss Brennan, still smiling from his funning remarks to her.

By now Kid and Slim were hooting and hollering full up cuz of her words and Ornery's reply. It was apparent to Miss Brennan that she was the butt-end of her very own words and a standing bit of humor that them there cowmen were so famous for.

She mustered her wits, her breath and her ire, and addressed Mr. O'Connor, "As you please, it will be…'Ornery'!" Ornery surprisingly replied, "She's a quick study." Kid answered, "Oh, and like ya' can't only half imagine. Ya' should ought see her with a revolver in her hand, Ornery!"

"Was that ya' two shootin' o'er here, in the pat hour?" queried Slim.

"Yep, that was we!" answered Kid.

"Us," Miss Brennan stated, "you mean 'us'".

"Yes, ma'am, us," replied Kid.

"Is she finally gonna make a readin' gent' outta ya'?" asked Ornery.

"She's gotta tough nut to crack with that one," stated Slim. Kid rolled his eyes as the rest funned him on his own account of the reading lesson and such stuff.

"Careful, boys," warned Miss Brennan, "he's got a fast gun!" She did a mock draw with her right hand and pointed index finger, like a mock shooter, pointing at Kid, "shooting" him with a warm smile.

Even Kid was laughing as Ornery and Slim mocked her draw and pointed their fingers at Kid. Kid pretended to be shot and fell in the dirt. Now the chuckling turned to hearty laughter. Slim was so very pleased to know it was this couple doing the shooting and not 'ne'er-do-wellers'. So Slim figured he'd live to see another day, and that was capitol news to his ears.

Ornery took to learning what brought them out to the overhang rock and so's they told him their story. He proceeded to invite them to come up and spend the night with them at their line shack. Guv to the lateness of the day, the teacher-lady and cow detective figured it a prudent thing to do. Miss Lisa told and Ornery looked after her horse's lamed hoof. Miss Lisa, Kid, and Slim worked to strike camp.

Ornery concluded Miss Brennan's mount was well enough to make the journey to the shack, if'n she rode onboard with Kid on his big horse. Ornery disclosed that once they reached the line shack he'd apply a healing horse liniment and make remedy of her animal, being's it was only minor. Slim took her book bag, while Ornery took her saddlebags, and as Kid made room for the two up on his seventeen and a half-hand high horse. And, in little time the boys and the little lady were making trail to ol' No. 7.

They took to going that day with only a few hours of daylight still on them. Ornery took the lead, Kid with Miss Lisa, and Slim followed up with Miss Brennan's empty-saddled horse trailing along on tether by Slim. As the train of four horses rode cross the high plains up into the short hills, Miss Brennan was enamored by her view from Kid's magnificently high horse.

The pair enjoyed the ride, the scenery, each other, her arms gently wrapped around Kid's waist. She contemplated the surrounding splendor of the uplands. Miss Lisa found joy in this ride, the day, and the conversation with her mavericker cow detective. Time to time she would rest her chin on Kid's shoulder as he talked in reply to her queries and comments.

As it was, Ornery thought they might have a mash, a crush, for each other, or was it calico fever he was a smelling from that pair. Alas, he wasn't no saw-bones so's to make any kind of diagnosis about a possible romance between these two. So he kept his words to his own, and Slim paid all this no-never-mind, pleasured in the peace of not having to shoot it out with no one, as he brought up the rear.

After two hours in the saddle they arrived at No. 7. And while it was by no means no hotel, all were in agreement it was a welcome picture to behold. Yet, Miss Brennan couldn't help notice the relatively fresh pock marked bullet holes all over the face of the little cabin. She stated, "Either this's Kid's handy work or someone sure got upset or bored. Look at all those bullet holes on the front of this place!" Ornery guv up a great big chuckle from hearing her words and Slim smiled from ear to ear trying hard to swallow his laughter so as not to risk hurting the lady's feelings.

Meanwhile, Kid turned his face back toward her and guvin' her a pleasantly polite dirty look and schemed his clever retort, "Ya' see 'em stray and misdirected pock marks there…there, and o'er there? Now that ain't my brand a shootin', 'Li'l Missy!'" Then he added, "I shoot a whole bit better than that…not like some greener, like 'em Double X boys and I thought ya' learn't that good about me today!"

"Learned," she replied skirting his main point, "the proper word is, 'learned'." "And, yes, I did learn that you shoot very, very well today."

As Slim and Ornery swung down from their mounts, Ornery went over to Kid's horse to assist the lovely schoolmarm down from her ride while Kid pondered both her shooting and grammar comments for some special meaning, beings she was a calico and all. Ornery said, "Miss Brennan, when ya' git to the Twenty Spread tomorrow, ya' be certain to query their *segundo*, Mr. Dutch Hammond about his shooting skills here on the O U T. Oh, and ask him fer me when's he comin' back and fix up No. 7, if'n ya' would?" Ornery flashed her a smile meaning she didn't have to ask anyone anything actually.

His words were his way of answering her query about who shot up the place. Between Kid and Ornery, they aided Miss Brennan down off the tall horse. She commented on what a lovely place the shack was located upon. Slim quickly interjected that he'd be pleasured to show Miss Lisa about the place when she was a mind to it. Both Ornery and Kid motioned them to go ahead on. They drew a light chuckle for Slim's sudden interest in their lady-friend and their alpine digs. The pair took to seeing about the small place.

The grand tour of N<u>o</u>. 7 wasn't lengthy, and before long the smell of fire in the stove and the pleasant aroma of supper wafted from the shack. Miss Lisa got supper cooking on the small stove and she turned her attention to her handbag, and the three lanterns in the cabin. From her reticule, at the cabin table, she fetched a small pair of snips. She took the lantern on the table, lifted the hood and fetched out the carbon stained glass globe. Next she fetched a used rag and wiped the globe soot free. With the snips she trimmed the carbon charred wick tip, replaced the globe piece back into the lantern and guv it to Slim. He proceeded to take the lantern outside and fill it with coal oil from a square tin container.

The two of them repeated this two more times until all three lanterns were ready for the coming evening. Slim was pleasured by her assistance with the evening chores, usually his, and a chore overdue.

Miss Brennan served the boys to a supper meal like was rarely served in the li'l shack. She tidied up as she went and Slim was sure she'd need to happen by more oft'. Once the boys had their fill of her flavorsome cooking they were all of the same judgment that a calico's touch had never graced this place ever, equally long overdue, highly appreciated, and much welcomed. The men pitched in and did up the rest of her chores for the night.

No sooner than the chores were done and Slim produced his harmonica and set to blowing up tunes for his pard and guests. He played old familiar tunes like "Ol' Susanna", "Yankee Doodle Dandy", and "Dixie". At the behest of their purdy calico houseguest, Slim played more tunes; "Amazing Grace", "(In the) Sweet By and By", "Shall We Gather at the River", and "The Battle Hymn o' the Republic". For sure Ornery's eyes got uppity some about that hymn, not being no kind of Yankee soul. He was a good host and held his tongue, except to say, "Ol' Buck Tussell!" That was his way of expressing his dislike about that tune. But it turned out to be a right fine evening of merriment anyway.

As bedtime come to the little shack the mavericker headed out for a spot to bunk down outside somewhere, just off the main path. The other cowmen decided Kid might ought to have company for the night. Of course, Miss Brennan protested mightily to the men for their being displaced from their home on her account, but the boys wouldn't have any of it. They made her prairie abode all set for the night. First, they built her a fine resting place, a comfy bunk. Then they fetched her in some fresh water and firewood for the coming morn. Lastly, they checked their shooters, as Ornery assured hers, "We're only a shout away should ya' need us." Famous last words thought Slim for some odd reason, not wanting to gunfight for his life in the dark, before they disappeared into that dark for the night.

What a day it had been for Miss Brennan, in her blessed manner, ending up off course, falling into the company of the O U T boys by meeting up with Yellowstone Kid and his swell company, and lastly for coming to be the first ever lady guest to come to this line shack home. There should be a prize for this event, she pondered with a self-smile. It shouldn't having taken an event like this, or even Christmas, to come on such fine company of good friends as this, this far from town. Yet, she was mighty grateful for this and for her friends, all of them about now. So's she drifted off to slumber-land she felt safe, secure and content, and slept deeply.

Struggling for air, Miss Lisa felt her night blouse extremely taunt at her neck. She felt her body being tugged at, slowly being pulled from her bed. Her ears detected light nail scratching, soft long grunting breaths like a near purring, and the smell of a feral beast, close, too close. An awful pain entered her left hand as she was dragged. Suddenly twisting, pulling and flaying her legs and free arm, she couldn't shake the pain or call out for aid. The beast jerked hard at her hand, not letting go its grip. As she hit the ground she laid face on face with a four-legged animal. Miss Lisa's shirt neckband gripped her throat bitterly and making noise came to not for her. All of a sudden it came upon her recollection that this was that very she mountain cat she had been attacked by and shot at earlier, she was rather certain of it.

At last the troubled maiden found her voice and screamed with pain as she wrestled to find her hand to her pillow and her small revolver. Again the cat bit and viciously now, on her forearm, and the blood came swift from her bite wound. She kicked and punched and rolled for life, rolling and now slipping in her own blood. Miss Lisa lost her grip on the bed and on any hope of retrieving her revolver. She was losing this battle, and rapidly.

A huge bright flash and blast washed over her and she felt the blast, the shock and heat; once, twice, a third time as Kid discharging his lever gun into the small cabin. Her ears rang and her eyes burned, she coughed, as the room now smothered in gun smoke that choked her. She felt the warm ooze of cat blood on her face and neck as it spattered about the place. Miss Lisa struggled to recover herself bared body and her bleeding wounds.

Slim ran inside, fumbled about the table so's to find a table lamp. He lit it, his revolver in hand. Ornery and Kid quickly hauled the dead cat from the roughed up, rattled and injured cabin mistress. Slim scrambled to pull a wooden box from the shelf near his bunk and went to the gal. Ornery said, "Slim, brin' me that light and guv me some water, then git the stove goin' and water on, fast."

"Lisa... Lisa... how're ya'?" called Kid. She nodded, not aware of how she was.

"Did ya' bar the door, how'd the cat git in here?" Ornery asked. He worked feverishly on Miss Brennan's wounded forearm and hand.

The boys worked tirelessly and finally managed to get the lady back into bed, mended, recuperating and her dead attacker removed from the shack. Miss Lisa lay resting; explained how she'd got a bit stuffy during the night and opened the door to get some air. Kid ruminated that the she cat was the one from earlier in the day, and then followed on to her lame pony. He was quite correct. With her bleeding stopped and the fresh water on, Ornery made good on her mending by cleansing her wounds up with hot water, his whiskey, examined her bruised neck and got the lady guest back off to sleep. Then the boys took turns watching over her and the equestrian stock until sun up.

On the morning, with one of Ornery's filling breakfasts under their belts, Kid redressed her wounds and assisted Miss Lisa into her day togs. He set up her horse and saddle for their intended, yet delayed destination. They prepared to take their leave of the O U T and ride to business at the Twenty Spread.

As they took to going, Kid turned to Miss Lisa, as they sat his horses and said, "Let's us be leavin' Cheyenne". Miss Brennan eyed Kid like she'd no notion of what he'd said. Ornery and Slim guv them a nod and tip of their hats as the pair commenced their departure.

Miss Lisa would not soon forget her summer's visit to ol' No. 7 line shack of the O U T. Also, she'd not soon disremember her outing with Ornery and Slim, their hospitality and the sharing of their small cabin home. Finally, there was her time with Kid and their time along the trail, and his stories of the past. As she went she recognized that even though she'd not gotten to her destination timely, she'd a gay time upon her unintended diversion. And, for that matter, what a grand time it had been for all of them that late summer's day on the Tucker spread of the prairie west. She wondered what they all pondered, what event would bring them back together like this again? Now there was telling of a forthcoming winter holiday and a life altering change for all, particularly Ornery and Slim.

# Chapter XII

## ORNERY AND SLIM'S VERY FIRST O U T CHRISTMAS

It was the Christmas season, actually, Slim's first on the O U T Spread. He really didn't know what to expect for sure. That's cuz Ornery, his partner of the last six months, wouldn't much say. What Slim discovered in the end would; scare, sober, show and satisfy both partners during this season of joy and love. But what were they both about to learn during this extraordinary season and about themselves?

Now it wasn't for the lack of trying that Slim had queried his partner as to the knowings and particulars of this special ranch event. And all he got for his effort to learn about an O U T Christmas was gruff mumbling and obvious dismissal from Ornery.

Other folk shared with Slim that Christmas was a crackerjack affair around the *rancho*. They revealed that Mr. Tucker 'throwed down' one heck of a fine shindig for the outfit, the local towns' folk, and their nearby neighbors. He did this as a way to guvin' thanks for the year's blessings and thanks to his hands and friends for a job well done. This also was to kick up the morale of the whole O U T Spread, beings it was winter, cold, dark and all.

The ritual went something like this; on Christmas Day the big house was transformed into a grand gala gathering of folks, food, and festivities. The big west wing of Mr. Tucker's southern colonial style ranch home was reconfigured into a ballroom and dining hall. Later, all of the local cattlemen, their top hands and choice folks from Well Springs would be received to attend this holiday hullabaloo.

The day prior, Mr. Tucker and Cap'n Stewart would see that each member of the outfit was granted a holiday bonus; usually gold coinage, beeves, special accoutrements or some such well-desired commodity. But it was the evening gathering which was the event of the year that all yearned for so fondly.

Slim was really beginning to get eager-ed up about the forthcoming holiday and the gathering of the whole O U T outfit, so's they might all be together like family. He was pleasured at the prospect of trading in his spurs and chaps for a crackerjack evening with his most fond favorite-d calico gal, Miss Denise Ellington. Slim realized he was gonna be attending Christmas far from his traditional home of Philadelphia, and this Christmas wouldn't be like any he'd ever experienced back east.

He smiled to himself as he thought this was a brand new event for both he and Miss Denise, to boot. Slim guessed they'd share another one of those new happenings like so much of this newfound life they'd been discovering, as a romancing couple, in partnership, having come all that far west together just that very same year.

His thoughts of being together at this new outfit for his very first cowmen's Christmas and dining and dancing with Miss Denise tickled Slim down to the core of his soul. And so much so, he'd a real tough time keeping his head in his chores. Ornery gladly consented to that fact as he kept getting on Slim to do so as they chore'd their way across the day's labors.

Not only was it Christmas on the Spread, but wintertime on the rolling prairies too. This was just another of the seasons when the livelihood of the outfit was about the upkeep of the winter herds. All of Mr. Tucker's leather-pounders were busy laboring from the section that was the big house right out to the farthest corners of the spread. The hired hands commenced to; mending fence wires, tacking up corral fence rails, cleaning stalls and horse stables, looking after the horse stock, and toiling to gather the winter herd to be watered and fed.

Some days the boys handled down snowdrifts around the place and kept the cattle trails opened to the stream, toughs and mangers. Other times there were cook shack and bunkhouse chores to do, like fetching of firewood or coal. Also, many a puncher was hard at it fixing up his riding gear and mending his togs while he was in possession of the spare time down to do so. So the ranch was a very active place in the winter, as Slim came to know.

To the outfit's favor this year was the fact that winter had been a gentle one across the Spread, at least up to the point just shy of Christmas. An icy cold norther, heavy with snow had come to their prairie home. The hands of the ranch were tasked with pushing all of the cow stock off the withering buffalo grass and back to the home place for better keeping.

The *segundo* guv the boys instruction to ride out to the far corners of the ranch to gather in the beeves that fell under their purview, O U T beeves or not, and trail them back to headquarters. Eight pairs of cow saddlers were dispatched from there, just a couple of days before Christmas day to gather the strays. Ornery and Slim were sent to the northwest corner to search out their share of doggies.

Slim was pleasured to getting out of the bunkhouse for a change and to be headed out that direction for this was territory most familiar to him, as it had been the very first ride he'd made shortly after his coming to the outfit. However, what wasn't familiar to him was this very same lay of the land in a heavy blanket of fresh snow, blowing wind and how queer it seemed to be all clad-ed up in his thick heavy winter garb of cotton, flannels, wools, and wooly animal hide outer clothing. He also wore a pair of pinto chaps pieced together from multi-colored pieces of different kinds of hair-covered hides.

Slim was grateful to have them bequeathed to him by a fellow in town who'd guv up the cow craft the season before he'd come. The thing that made him most uncomfortable was that scratchy wool muffler that he needed to wrap about his head and face for protection from the driving snow filled wind. Slim was certain that he'd simply perish for that lack of wind to breath now that he was all bedeviled, like being entombed inside his full winter garb. Slim reckoned he weighed an extra twenty pounds for all the extra duds.

Ornery was garbed up in his grizzlies, a buffalo robe coat, a beaver hat, and badger mittens to keep warm and dry from the elements. Laughing himself good, as he gazed upon his young bunkie, he said, "Hey, Slim, ya'll git used to 'em duds, cuz it's better than freezin' to death an' bein' wind blown ice solid." The snow continued to fall as they rode out and away from the home place. Slim begun to ponder what kind of Christmas adventure lay before them just about now?

Well, as it all played out for those cow-saddlers, after two miserably cold days of a late season roundup, in stiff winds and tall drifts of snow, finally brought the last of the strays back home. Ornery and Slim were the last pair to ride in cuz Slim was still a greener. As they rode up to the barn at headquarters, just beyond the little citadel, in the very early evening, both men did appear like 'snowmen on horseback'. Their dark coats, chaps, mitts, and face wraps were laden thick with a frozen layer of wind packed snowy glazed ice.

Ornery watched with some curiosity as his bunkie attempted his best to lift himself up and out of his riding rig in a dismount, weighed down in ice as he was. However, before he could call out a timely warning, Slim tipped over his saddle and wrecked hard onto the snow-covered earth right next to his horse. The horse never flinched nary a muscle and only looked down at the cowman, with relief, to be loosed off of Slim's frozen mass of weight. Ornery carefully climbed off his horse, executed a dismount technique that took into account the ten or more pounds of weight he'd gained from his snow and ice laden winter gear.

Once on the ground, he knocked some of the snow and ice from his outer wear. He trudged over to where Slim lay on his back, staring up in a dazed and abashed disbelief for his turn of events. Slim obviously disremembered Ornery's earlier warning about maneuvering around in snow laden wooly-clothes. Ornery peered down at his partner, smiled shaking his head in wonderment.

"Slim, ya' ailin' much?"

"No, I reckon my thick coat and this fresh snow bed here busted my fall purdy swell." Then asking, half in jest and half not, "Where'd all that weight come from, Ornery?" Ornery did his best not to laugh in the youngster's face, so's he turned away, thinking his pard a slowpoke cowpoke. Ornery explained, "It's that whole day's collection of snow and ice on yer coat and wooly chaps that I cautioned ya' about that got ya' cha all off balance during yer dismount." Slim nodded, un-disremembering what Ornery had shared upon his ears earlier that very same day. Slim reached out his hand for Ornery's helping grip so's to aid him back upright to his boots once more.

Now Ornery declared, "Let's git 'em ponies squared up so's we can go put the feedbag on o'er at the big house as Mister Tucker's 'pectin' us there before dark, since it's Christmas Eve, and all!" The two snow laden saddlers lead their horses through the barn door and into the stables as the snow came down, as the day wore down to not. They finished up caring for their horses as was their manner and headed straight away to the main house to join the rest of the outfit for supper.

Once Ornery and Slim was inside, and off with their winter duds, they were warmly greeted and made welcome to the large dining room table now covered heavily in a holiday feast. Ornery was pleasured to be gathered, once more, at this customary table with all of his familiar work mates. Some he'd not seen in days or longer for that matter. Yet the pleasure he wasn't having was that of being reminded about this time of year for which he'd little or no use of my memory. Yet, in spite of that he came as social tradition on the Spread dictated.

Slim was overwhelmed to witness all of the holiday grandeur of this room and the entire banquet spread out before him. He wasn't for certain, for certain, when he'd ever seen so much vittles in one place at the same time. The smells inside caused his tummy to wiggle with joy and hunger, and his mouth to water good for the thought of feasting so luxuriously. He was just sure and for certain he'd died and gone to cowman's cook shack heaven for the feast that awaited him there. Here was a partnership he'd nigh on missed there at the Tucker table himself and the fair food feast of a lifetime.

Mr. Tucker pleasantly greeted the pair with holiday salutations and invited them to join the rest of the family at the table. After Mr. Tucker guv the supper blessing and nod, and the entire outfit took to the feast set before them. In time the table's company commenced in sharing stories of blessing guv them or a favorite story of the past year, or two. Silently Slim sat back eating this most excellent supper of; mashed potatoes and beef gravy, wild turkey, beef, bread stuffing, green beans, sweet potatoes, cranberry sauce, bread pudding, dinner rolls, pumpkin pie and more, all while 'feasting' on more of the evening tales and traditions going on around him. This was the 'Christmas' before Christmas he done figured. He wondered why Ornery wouldn't tell of such things.

With supper finished Mr. Tucker asked Cap'n Stewart to guv holiday bonuses out to every member of the outfit and Mr. Tucker shared his words of gratitude and holiday cheer up his outfit as the evening wore down to night. With that, some of the crew stayed on in the drawing room while other headed back for the bunkhouse. Ornery and Slim, plum tuckered and ready for a good night's slumber, turned in, cuz all the boys had a full day ahead of them on the morrow… Christmas Day.

Now Christmas day started with a magnificently bright sunrise and the promise of a beautifully sun filled day, following days of overcast skies and blinding wind and snow. The atmosphere was cold and crisp, and it was clear blue sky all the way to the horizon and back. Chores and chuck were the first order of the day.

In the bunkhouse Slim got to his togs and boots so's to go choring. He discovered Ornery was no place to be found and that confounded him a bit as Ornery was rare to leave out without saying his business first. How-some-ever, this whole Christmas ordeal had Ornery acting queer-some anyways. "No bother," murmured Slim. It was Christmas day; the day of the big *rancho* gala, the visiting townsfolk, more food, and the long awaited eve of song and Epicurean* pleasure with his Miss Denise and new friends.

Slim took to chores, all caught up in the merriment of the day, when suddenly Hap come to him and said, "Yo, Slim, ya'd best git up to the big house cuz the *segundo* wants you, pronto."

"Why, am I in trouble?"

"Don't know Slim, but go now, cuz the Cap'n's a man ya' don't keep waitin'."

Hap's words swiftly reminded him of Ornery's warning never to make no one in the outfit be kept waiting, especially the *segundo*.

And again Slim was tossed for a loop that morning by this seemingly odd request or order as it was. First, Ornery went off without saying anything to no one, and now this trip up to the foreman. Slim had never been summoned, by name, to the main house before. He stopped, dusted off a bit and trotted up to headquarters to meet with the man.

When Slim arrived up at the big house, Augustus, Mr. Tucker's hired Negro house-attendant met him in the foyer of the parlor room.

"Good mornin' and Merry Christmas to ya' Augustus," Slim said with a big grin on his freshly frosted face.

"A good day and Merry Christmas to ya', too, Mista. Sleem!" Augustus cheerfully replied. "If'n ya'll have a chair the Cap'n will be with ya' shortly, Mista Sleem." Slim smiling, politely nodded, yet remained standing fearing he was too soiled to touch any of the fine cloth parlor furniture.

Augustus departed the foyer straight away to go fetch the Cap'n. Slim just stared about the walls of foyer at the wonderfully decorated entryway, it being decked out in total holiday splendor. Slim turned about and peered out the window across the yard. As he gazed on the big yard, the one he'd just come in from, it was the long sets of rope guidelines that ran around that same yard that grabbed his attention.

The lines had been placed there in late autumn to aid the men in traveling from building to building along the yard whenever the snow and blizzard winds made it impossible to visually navigate around big yard. Slim wasn't certain he'd want to be learned about going in blizzards for the storms that Ornery told of nearly scared him from his wits just for the thought of them. Slim quietly pondered how very different his new home was compared to the one he'd left behind, in Philly, less than a year ago. Under his breath, Slim said, "Everythin' here's so much more of an adventure than back home." And in fact it truly was.

In a matter of minutes Mr. Tucker and Cap'n Stewart came to the foyer to greet Slim who was standing by, nervously. It was the boss first, "Merry Christmas, Mr. Slimmery. How are you enjoying life with us here in Wyoming? Slim shyly answered, "Really swell, sir, thank ya' fer asking." He was hoping he wasn't going to be asked to leave off the Spread. After a moment Mr. Tucker said, "Captain has some words for you, so I'll leave him to do just that. Good day puncher." Slim replied, "Yes sir, thank ya', and Merry Christmas." He left the parlor and now it was the Cap'n's turn, "Slim, I need you to fetch yer winter gear, saddle up and leave off the Spread. You won't need to wait for Ornery because he's gone too." In a flash Slim understood why Ornery hadn't much said to him after supper or why he wasn't around this morning. He didn't want to be around when Slim was run off the outfit. His heart sank, what was he going do or tell Miss Denise, and on Christmas Day of all times, why now? Well at least he had his Christmas bonus of gold coinage to tide him over for a time until he could find up another outfit needing a cowpuncher, or fetch a ride going back home if'n it came down to it. His heart sank for the thought of having to leave.

Cap'n Stewart continued, "Mister Tucker needs you to leave off to town to escort his friends and special guests out here to the ranch for the Christmas Day eve fiesta. I've a choice list of chores I need accomplish and for you to be off to town within the hour." Slim was suddenly so excited, "Yer not quitting me off the brand, sir?" Cap'n eyed Slim inquisitively.

"No, I just need you in town, that's all. Why? Where did ya' think I wanted ya'?"

"Nowhere, but town, as ya' requested and to have our guests back here, that's all.

"Capital, lad! Let us be ta doin' it," the Cap'n replied.

It was this special chore and the details of its timely execution that Slim figured he'd badly mis-under-took, misunderstood, as the Cap'n spake to Slim's leaving. All of this change of routine and the holiday excitement had Slim not thinking so straight or hearing straight. This just going of the chore was so much better than getting throwed of the Spread, so he figured.

All a sudden Hap burst through the main door and into the foyer, having come from the big yard, in a panic, "Empty saddle in the yard, Cap'n!" The room fell immediately silent as his words struck their ears. Those were fear-provoking words and brought an awful harsh chill to every saddler whoever heard them spake. This meant a rider was afoot, perhaps injured, or worse, dry gulched and left for buzzard bait, dead or dying. This empty saddle stuff was never a welcome sign for saddlers anytime, anywhere, but especially not during this time of year, guv the cold, the snow and limited amount of total daylight available.

Joined by Mr. Tucker, the four men raced out on to the porch to fetch a look at the rider-less saddle mount. They swiftly recognized the big quarter horse and riding rig to be that of Ornery's. Cap'n Stewart spake first, "O'Connor's no untried pistol, so's his bein' outta da saddle could only spell us real trouble." Every man standing there acknowledged that Ornery was that, a top cowhand extraordinaire, and agreed with Cap'n words, both verbally and mentally.

Cap'n Stewart told of Ornery's being dispatched to town very early that morning on official ranch business and a personal errand. He was to meet up later in the day with Slim, Roy Covington, Charlie Spragg, and Chance Yocum. It was from town the five saddlers would escort their ranch guests back to the home place.

Cap'n and Slim went out to Ornery's mount to look for signs of whatever might have become of him. At a glance of the rig, Ornery's beloved Henry lever gun was missing from the rifle boot and his winter wool wrap-blanket, the one normally tied down up under the cantle, was gone too. The horse was going like it had an injured Indian flank-side. Something had gone really wrong for Ornery, cuz he'd go to boot hill before he'd guv away his horse and riding rig, thought Slim. He'd un-disremembered Ornery telling him that on more than one occasion.

The Cap'n ordered Slim and Hap to make their horses and a buckboard ready to go, swiftly. Cap'n formed his posse to go out to find Ornery, and in fewer than twenty minutes the rescue party was out in front of the big house, as ordered. Mr. Tucker bade his outfit, "Good hunting and Godspeed," as Kid, Kit, Roy, Hap, Cyrus, Pat and Slim mounted up and rode off the home place. Tom Gardner and Moze took the buckboard and followed on behind the mounted riders directly.

With the fresh snow and bright sunlight the party didn't even have to leave off the big yard to follow the set of hooves prints back to their origin. Tracks made fresh in the new snow, a set of tracks going away and a set of tracks coming back in, fresher than the ones going out. Of course both sets were from Ornery's stallion. Half an hour out from the ranch the tracks veered off the trail going strangely south. In places there was plenty of snow on the ground, but fortunately it wasn't but a foot or two deep in most places, as they followed the tracks.

It became apparent to the searchers that Ornery wasn't any longer going toward town, being he was now far from the main road, or so the evidence did tell on him. Also, the tracks swung wide and deeper south of that road, as the evidence wandered around snowdrifts and headed off in no direct line to any point that made any cowhand sense to any of them. Cap'n Stewart and party noticed Ornery's tracks cut hard in spots like a crazy man, or someone playing cat and mouse or some such senseless game.

Then the tracks went off in even larger circles and then doubled back on the searchers, like a *loco* man or a man trying to outmaneuver a great ghost. Cap'n Stewart had Moze keep the wagon up near the main trail to wait until they located Ornery, or his remains, for fear of busting up the buckboard or tuckering out the team. Cap'n headed his search party along the snow-covered tracks, again, in pursuit of Patrick O'Connor.

Sometime later, it was Kid that glimpsed sight of another set of much different looking tracks that attempted to intersect those of Ornery's horse. He rode off in that direction to investigate, Slim on behind him. The tracks intersected a number of times showing a great upheaval in the snowy surface cover and guv off the appearance that the two sets of tracks were engaged in some kind of wild dance around and about in the snow, one after the other.

From the hoof prints and track pattern he saw, Kid was certain Ornery was still up his the saddle when these tracks were made. It was the other tracks in the snow that guv Kid a belly tickling start when he finally recognized them to be a Grizzly Bear. If it was, things really did not look swell for Ornery. When Hap pointed out to the crimson colored stains in the snow, just before the rise out in front of the rescue party, concern was everyone's suddenly.

Instantaneously all the saddlers pulled their rifles or revolvers in the anticipation of what was waiting them just over the other side of that hilltop. Cap'n Stewart motioned to the men to fan out and approach the hilltop abreast of the ridge. As they did they found the ugly, messy source of the blood and gore.

It was Ornery all right, his blanket, his rifle and himself covered in blood from what could be made of him from where they were. How sad, and on Christmas Day. Slim's heart sang again for the second time that day. His mind raced to recall all of the memories of Ornery and of all the warnings Ornery had shared on him of the perils that could kill a man while saddle pounding. He didn't recall a bear mauling as one of them, though it did make good sense and all. Then there was the bear there, all covered in blood too. As the rescue party peered down from where they sat saddled it was a matter of opinion of who had gotten it worse, the Grizzle bear, or ol' Ornery. And, the long and short of it was the bear was quite dead, thanks to Ornery, and Ornery mostly wasn't, or at least not quite yet. Regrettably this seen looked more like a job for Well Spring's undertaker, Mercer than for a cattleman's rescue party.

Ornery ailing badly, battered, a bit bloody and froze good, was still clinging to life. The blood was on and around the bear mostly. The worst Ornery suffered was cold exposure, an aching body from the fall from his horse, along with an ailing pride for not being able to out fox that powerful bruin all while being dethroned from his pony. But Ornery wasn't out of the woods, so to speak, needing doctoring and all warm sanctuary of solace.

Ornery, alive, was the first of many presents received on Slim and him that day. Lying on his blanket in the snow, a dead bear at his feet, his lever gun shot dry and spent forty-four (.44 Henry) rim-fire cartridge cases strewn all about him, Ornery was doubly relieved, having found rescue, a second present. In poor health, Ornery gingerly shared words of gratitude with Cap'n Stewart and Slim, as they, the first two riders, come to be by his side. Ornery said, "I'm pleasured to have retained my rifle and blanket from off my run away mount as we wrecked with that bear. Fer it t'was all that kept me goin', along with my wits." Cap'n Stewart ordered Kit to go fetch the wagon to where they was, now that they'd found their wrecked saddler.

Ornery asked, "How's my ride, is he still livin'?" Slim answered, "Ornery, don't fret, he's doing better than ya' fer he's already stabled, bedded down and that's more than we can say fer ya'." Cap'n had to agree with Slim, as they prepared to fetch away the bummed up saddler. When the wagon arrived; Kit, Slim, Kid, and Moze fetched Ornery up inside, wrapping him in several wool blankets and pillowed his head. Once loaded up and made comfortable for transport, he was taken home. The Cap'n and Kid escorted the buckboard back to the ranch.

The rest of the party rode for Well Springs to meet the holiday guests, including; Doc. Bannon, Preacher Dixson, Marshal Summerville, Mr. Ellington, Miss Ellington, Miss Brennan, and Miss Emory, among others. Before they went, Slim rode next to the wagon eyeing Ornery, his head and heart struggling in an emotional tug-of-war fearing he'd not see Ornery live again if he departed him just this now. He truly wanted to go to town to personally escort Miss Ellington and the others back. However, he sorely felt he belonged at his pard side, to see him safely home. Slim knew Ornery would have done the same if'n the situation was turned about.

Ornery took stock in Slim's persistence to deliver him home and slowly motioned Slim that he should go and finish what he had started, "the boss's orders" and that's what truly needed to be done. Ornery weakly mumbled, "No cowman's worth his salt if'n he's not good on his words and doin's, so git after yer chorin'." And off they did go.

Much later on the day, all was peaceful at the big house of the O U T Spread, as the holiday festivities took hold of the place. Ornery had survived his buckboard ride to the home place and was no worse for the wear for his day's ordeal. Augustus had stripped Ornery of his frozen clothing. They warmed, dried, and bedded him down in an upstairs bedroom at the main house. He was grubbed up with some of Coosie's special healing hot beef broth. Ornery was left to rest and recoup while awaiting Doc Bannon's visit. He'd been doted on a plenty by Mr. Tucker and the house staff, and left to fetch a much-deserved recuperative nap.

Meantime, Slim's delegation rode to town, and once there retrieved the items from the Cap'n list. Then they escorted the guests and doctor out to the big house, in fine holiday fashion, caroling along the way. When this party arrived to the ranch and was safely in from the cold, they unwrapped from their winter attire. They all warmed by the fireplace in the drawing room, and partook of tummy warming beverages. And soon the place was a hum and buzz with holiday chat, cheer, and cozy clamor, as all gathered around in west wing for the evening.

Slim and the other boys cleaned up incredibly respectable and made a welcome addition to the crowd. Ornery was made ready and came downstairs aided by the pleasant assistance of Miss Shannon. Their entry lent to the makings of a fine Christmas party, one grand and full of blessings and holiday cheer. As Ornery entered the dining hall and ballroom of the west wing he discovered, as he suspected, both Miss Denise and Slim leading the company in a chorus of, *Silent Night*. Miss Shannon stood next along side Miss Denise, Slim, and Miss Lisa and Kid, all singing along with the rest of the houseguests.

As he was glimpsed entering in, the singing ceased as the folks in the room burst out into a rousing cheer for the drained and dinged up, but freshly restored cowman hero of the evening. Even with all of the fanfare Ornery truly didn't feel like any kind of a hero. As everyone gathered around him they shook his hand and wishing him swift recovery, and sharing holiday salutations upon him, Ornery felt a bit overwhelmed and self conscious for all of the extra attention. Everyone admired Ornery for his dashing dark-silver suit and Miss Shannon's lovely silver-satin dress. She gingerly tucked herself in by his side and guv him a quick kiss for which he so shyly received, but appreciated. Again, the room broke into an affectionate cheer for this couple.

Others were festively appareled like Miss Lisa wearing a holiday colored plaid ball dress, plaid-ed in red, green with fine thin lines of white and black setting off the red and green. Kid wore a smartly dressed tailored dark-brown suit. They stood closely together, side by side, the backside of her left hand very much touching the backside of Kid's right hand, both wearing smiles of joy and looking on with glee. Standing a bit removed from the circle of folks; Miss Denise was clothed in a celebratory dark emerald green ball gown and Slim in a charcoal gray tailor-made suit. They stood arm-in-arm appearing lovingly cozy. They smiled a smile of happiness for their friends. They were so pleasured to see Ornery up and about, and with Miss Shannon, to boot.

After a time Mr. Tucker invited his houseguests to be seated for Christmas supper, and sit they did to a very, very long meal set table with especially fine chinaware and silver set from England. Preacher Dixson blessed the supper meal with words of thanksgiving. Mr. Tucker sat, guv his nod, and all commenced with Christmas supper. Now plenty of conversation, the passing of food dishes, and the clatter of silver on good china filled the room.

When everyone had their fill of Coosie's grand feast, the talk around the table turned to Cap'n Stewart who queried, "If'n ya'd be so kind Mr. O'Connor and share with us all about your mornin' ride?"

"Well Cap'n," replied Ornery, "it's a purdy tedious tale to tell on a lovely occasion such as this, sir."

"Oh please, tell away, Patrick!" pressed the Cap'n, as did others present. Flush with feelings of embarrassment, Ornery looked upon all of the faces now peering at him.

Ornery reluctantly agreed to tell his tale to everyone there, "I saddled Blackie and left off the big yard going along the snowy road to town. I rode the main trail nigh on thirty minutes in the early morning light and cold crisp clear air o' the same. As I reached the southern point on the trail, goin' east, I'z caught a glimpse to me left o' a big brown mound in the midst o' the snow covered prairie, about 50 yards out. It was about then that Blackie, whose nostrils was frosted up from the crisp cold air, let go a sneeze. All the same sudden that snow-based brown mound whirled about and rose up on its hind legs from the level, sniffing the air, and I eyes looked me a grizzle bear fer dead certain. In a flash, I swiftly veered off of me goin' east trail fer goin' swift south as I turned me a wide circle on me way back to the *rancho*. Goin' where I did I turned Blackie due south and dashed outta sight o' the bear, disappearin' behind the crest o' a mild slope.

That grizzle bear bein's all ready fer a Christmas meal, I figured, guv to a hard charge, south, at me, cuz he could sniff me and my fleeing pony. Surely like, that bear bound o'er the trail until he caught sight o' his holiday feast an' come on us lively."

This explicated plenty to why Ornery's Blackie and the bear tracks created that strange 'dance' pattern, the rescue party discovered in the snow earlier that day, as the horse and rider tried to elude their attacker.

Ornery continued, "At the bottom end o' our dance with the bear an' me; twistin', cuttin', and turnin' the four-legged beasts came together in a nasty collision. As weez run into t'other we all tipped o'er. I'z tipped off my riding rig; I hurriedly plucked off my rifle and snatched my blanket clean. I wrecked to the snow, hard and landed where ya' found me.

Now 'em two animals found their legs, Blackie first an' gittin' off to a fair lead on the fiercely famished bruin. He headed swiftly for *rancho*, and direct like. My rider-less pony promptly put a gap between himself and the bear. Both animals rapidly left me, head-numb thar on the prairie floor. In the rush to catch his equestrian eats, the grizzly didn't even notice I was crashed off. Heavy with gear, I struck the ground so hard it knocked me wind part out, as I bounced off the snow I found time to fetch my firearm and all as I watched Blackie goin' plum gone. And best as I could tell, near seventy yards north by west o' me, which bruin stuff abruptly halted and nearly tipped o'er. He rose to his hind legs an' stood upright, twisted about, sniffing the air discernin' an easier meal, an' so much closer too."

Ornery continued, "Layin' there, I propped up against a boulder as I hastily fumbled about in my lower buffalo coat pocket fer more Henry cartridges. Loadin' up my rifle up, and cuttin' a fast glance at that bear, I eyed him still standing tall. I'z care-some like set my long gun to my achin' shoulder an' propped the barrel a top my left knee. Swift and steadily I took to smokin' that big bear with eight rounds into his upper form from just his comin' o'er that slight rise in the rollin' 'scape.

Amidst the crisp brightness, the rifle smoke hung thick on me an' my burnin' achin' eyes. I struggled through cold, smoke tear filled eyes to see as that big beast swatted wildly at those heavy bee stings I was placin' upon at his upper body. Then he hauled off an' bolted at me, the author of those lead heavily made bees. Fast, I shot and shot and shot, but don't rememorate much else after that." And what he did recall was later; he found holding his Colt revolver and covered by that blanket. The bear found quite dead at Ornery's feet bled out on the snow, and on Ornery's blanket. Ornery figured later, after he was rescued, clinging to life, that this was a blessing from the 'Man' above. And, everyone knew what happened after that.

Gripped by a curious recall of thought Slim interrupted the moment to ask, "What's it that 'em bears come by when it's winter?"

"Hibernation," young Wyatt replied, "it's called hibernation, Slim."

"So why didn't that bear do that what Wyatt send, if'n it was winter an' all?" queried Slim. Ornery commenced to explicate by what and how the bear population did such an activity as such, sharing that if the bear wasn't prepared to go into hibernation, which they don't truly hibernate in the full or true sense of the word, or could still find food to feast on. Ornery offered, "Well it wouldn't hide in no hole if'n it can go on feasting." And that was Slim's swell answer.

With his story told, everyone left the dining room table to gather about the generously decorated Christmas tree near the piano across the large room. Slim caught Ornery's arm and gingerly said, "Was ya' in fear fer ya' life durin' all that bear ordeal?" Ornery, suddenly sporting a Cheshire cat grin said softly so's not to catch the calico's ears, "I'm in fear of only two thin's lad, endin' up on my feet, and an honest woman. But, ya' ne'er heard that from me, ya' hear?" Then they found their calicos; they went off to the west wing with the rest. And once the gala party settled about the brilliantly decorated tree; Mr. Tucker guv recitation most eloquently from the Book of Luke, and to the birth of the Christ-Child Story, and then they commenced to pass around brightly wrap gifts while sharing many stories of Christmas' of bygone years so's to pass the magnificent evening.

Miss Denise and Slim were so pleasured to be together, again, with friends, who were like a family now, as they shared their first Christmas at the O U T Spread, on the western prairie. This whole evening was a little frontier heaven on which to behold, now and forever more. Slim and Denise easily coaxed the gathering into singing more holiday hymns. And this was just another example of how the folk that lived ranch life in those days of the cowman's west, the 'Cowmen-Christmas Spirit', in a modest kind of way of taming their western frontier, with peace.

To the good fortune of Ornery and his trusty "Henry" rifle, he'd provided at the last moment the roast bear in addition to the evening's supper fare. Ornery also promised Slim a new pair of wooly chaps of bear hide, no less. The bear meat meal and the bear hide chaps, when they got made, would be another fine set of presents made out of that Christmas season. Thanks to Mr. Tucker and the outfit's swift rescue of Ornery, Slim still had his favorite partner for another day of chores and mentorship on the *rancho*.

For this holiday *fiesta,* Ornery and Slim, and their company, had the pleasure of a very fine evening like they, as a team, had never known. These were friends, like family, which wad something Slim had little experience growing up with as an orphan. Ornery's long time denial of basic human goodness and human joy pushed him away from a holiday family for many years, nigh on his self imposed tradition, this denial up until Slim. No Christmas in Philadelphia, or any place, might have been more joyous for these two and their friends. They quickly recognized all of this to be a real Christmas blessing and the true reason for this season, like none before, for them at the O U T Spread.

Seemingly Ornery's young partner and Slim's confounded fascination with family and Christmas was honestly on to something after all. For the first time since Ornery lost his dearly beloved, Miss Charlotte, at Christmas, back in '62, nigh on twenty year ago, could he finally started looking past the pain; the hurt, agony and the ugly personal loss of that derned war and her tragic and untimely death. Ornery had to put past him his distrust of that hideous side of humanity that he'd witnessed all those years ago. At present he might open his heart, once more, and let in the joy of this season, now that he finally found a truly fine reason for doing so during this truly caring season.

So thanks to the goodness bestowed on him, when he required it most, from friends, the boss, the outfit, and townsfolk, his disdain for Christmas was now no longer. Ornery counted himself a bountifully blessed man and this he counted for plenty. His discovery of the full O U T spirit of Christmas and of his friends, on Christmas Day no less, spared his very life, filled him up with new found realization of love and respect for this very special time of year. So this was Ornery's first, real O U T Christmas, after all.

Slim was as equally gratified that Ornery's life had been saved. His Christmas blessings were a long list that began the moment he'd first started for the O U T and building all of these partnerships. First with Miss Denise Ellington and all she brought to his life. Second was with Mr. Tucker, Cap'n Stewart and the rest of the outfit. Finally, his partner, Ornery, and all the lessons he'd learned upon Slim. Yes, even when Ornery was being just plain ornery. This made 'no never mind' to Slim by now, for this kind of Christmas was enough for him for now. And, no better gifts could be guv him, except maybe, heaven, guv to him from the Lord, Himself.

This then was Ornery and Slim's very first O U T Christmas, wonderful and first-rate. A blend of blessings to numerous to name; in the 'land of free and the home of the brave,' of being cowmen living free in the greatest nation on Earth, by the grace of God so's they did figure.

Nonetheless, this first Christmas wasn't, at all, the end of trail for either Ornery and Slim, but the long rode to a lifetime of partnership that had began because of their prairie life on the O U T Spread. What would they be on to doing next, well; they'd have to come to that once they were back in the saddle again.  Go good!

# GLOSSARY

**1st Model Winchester 1866:** See "Yellow Boy" lever rifle.

**.45-110/.45-70/.45-90:** blackpowder cartridges having a 45/100s of an inch diameter lead projectile/bullet. Also, a brass or copper centerfire case, primer in the center of the case base, sized to be filled with 110/70/90 grains of blackpowder. For improved accuracy some projectiles were partially wrapped about the lead projectile base and lower body with very fine paper and were referred to as, 'paper-patched bullets'.

**'71-72 'Open-Top' Colt revolver:** The Model 1871-72 Colt revolvers, produced as a new design of Colt metallic cartridge revolver fashioned on but different from 1851 Navy and 1860 Army blackpowder, percussion revolvers chambered initially in the caliber, Henry .44 Rimfire, later in .32 and .38 Colt.

**Absaroka:** See Crow Indians.

**Airtights:** Tin canned foods, or foods in tin cans.

**Arbuckles:** Old west for a new, green or brand new cowhand. Also, a famed prairie, ranch and chuckwagon utilized brand of coffee available since 1865 until today. T came with a stick of peppermint candy enclosed in the packaged product.

**Arikara Indians:** North American, (USA) plains natives forming the northern group of the Caddoan language family. Their language differs only in dialect from the Pawnees. The Arikara left the Pawnee, associated with the Skidi. Lewis and Clark met the tribe in 1804. They, (Lewis and Clark) spoke of Arikara as the remnant of 10 powerful Pawnee tribes living in 1804, in 3 separate villages. Due to disease and war these villages were heavily reduced and little remains of their former greater tribal divisions. The Arikara became close neighbors with, and eventually allied with the Mandan and Hidatsa tribes. At the treaty drawn up at Ft Laramie, Wyoming Territory, in 1851 with the US military, the Arikara, Mandan, and Hidatsa, the land claimed by these tribes was/is described as lying west of the Missouri, from Heart River, Dakota Territory (N.D.), to the Yellowstone River, and up the latter to the mouth of Powder River, Montana Territory, thence southeast to the headwaters of the Little Missouri River, in Wyoming, Territory.

**Bandito:** (Spanish) Bandit, thief or outlaw.

**Belly wash:** coffee or 'Arbuckles'.

**Big windy:** Tall tale or story

**Bob-wire:** Cowboy for, barbed wire, a style of braided wire with barbs or sharp shaped metal pieces of wire built into the twisted or braided strands of wire and used as a fencing material to pen in livestock, or keep out various other undesirable entities. An invention usually given credit to one Joseph F. Glidden and his patent of 1873.

**Boss of the Plains:** The famed hat designed by *John B. Steton.*

**Buck-the-Tiger:** To gamble, deal or go against advisable odds.

**Bunkie:** Slang for *bunkhouse* partner.

**Buckaroo(s):** Anglicized from the Spanish, *vaquero(s)*, meaning "cowman".

**Buffalo grass:** The grass of the prairie where the buffalo fed.

Cabello: (Spanish, caw-by`-oh) horse.

**Calico(s):** Printed cotton fabric worn by women, also a substitute term for women by the men in the west.

**Calico fever:** Being in love or having special feelings for another one of the opposite gender.

**Cannoneer:** An artilleryman.

**Cantle**: The raised rear portion of a saddle seat.

**Caisson and Limber:** Two-wheeled vehicle for artillery ammunition and two-wheel gun/cannon carriage, usually horse-drawn.

**Cayuse** (kii-yous): Small native range horse, said to have a mind of their own, ornery.

**Cheyennes,** (Northern, in the context of Ornery and Slim, 1861 to 1900), The Northern Cheyenne were (are) a sub-part nation of Native American Plains Indians. Their name 'Cheyenne' is derived from the Lakota Sioux for, 'Little Cree'. Famous among the Plains Indians, they were highly warlike and notable horseman. The Cheyenne were allied to the Arapaho and Lakota nations. The Northern Cheyennes broke off from and located with the Western Sioux nation near the Black Hills, in the Dakota Territory and the Wyoming Territory. Chief Dull Knife (Tah-me-la-pash-me) and his Northern Cheyennes did battle alongside Lakota and Arapaho in the destruction of Colonel George Armstrong Custer and most of the US 7th Cavalrymen at what would become known as, 'Custer's Last Stand' or 'Battle of the Little Bighorn' (Greasy Grass River), Montana Territory in June 1876. Today, the Northern Cheyenne live in southeast Montana on the Northern Cheyenne Indian Reservation, located about the small communities of Lame Deer and Ashland, Montana. Their reservation borders the Crow Indian Reservation in Montana, as well.

**Cheyenne Roll Saddle:** A saddle type made by saddle maker Frank Meanea of Cheyenne and quite popular in the 1870's and '80's with the range riding cowmen.

**Chuck:** Food, chow, grub.

**Colt '73 Cavalry:** The Colt 1873 Army model revolver with a 7-1/2" barrel.

**Coosie:** (koo-see): Old west slang from the Spanish for, *cocinero* or cook.

**Cotton:** Not in agreement with or in favor of.

**Cow Detective:** Regulator, gun for hire/hired gun contracted by a ranch owner or a group of ranches to help protect ranch assets from outlaw activities and encroachers upon the ranch property, free grazers, sod busters, sheep herds, etc.

**Crow: or Absaroka:** (In the context of Ornery and Slim, 1861 to 1900), Native American tribe, in times gone by, lived in the Yellowstone River Valley of Montana. Rivals to the Lakota and Arikara Indians, and allied with the US Military, (e.g., Colonel George Armstrong Custer's US Seventh Calvary). Present day, the tribal headquarters are located at Crow Agency, Montana, USA.

**Chronometer, vest pouch**: Pocket timepiece or pocket watch

**Dally or Dallied:** Anglicized Spanish (*Dar la vuelta* give a turn), or to wrap around, the saddle horn with a lariat or rope.

**Doggies:** Calf or calves, sometimes applied to yearling cows, or the herd in general.

**Dinner:** The mid-day meal. Supper is the evening meal to westerns of the period.

**Disremember**: To forget

**Double X:** (slang) The ranch known as the, "XX Spread" or "Twenty Spread, and neighbor spread to the west southwest of the O U T Spread. See, Twenty Spread or XX Spread.

**Dry gulch**: To ambush, bushwhack or kill.

**Epicurean(s):** Followers of a philosophy of modest or noble pleasure as described by the Greek philosopher, *Epicurus*, (341 to 270 BC).

**Fatback**: Bacon, in this context.

**Feedbag:** A device attached to the head of livestock for feeding. Here it means to go eat.

**Filch:** Steal, take, or run off with.
**Fun** or **Funned**: To tease or kid

**Greener** or **green**: A brand new person in this context, also a brand name of a shotgun.

**Grizzlies**: Grizzly bear chaps

Hacienda (Spanish): In this book, the home or house of the ranch owner.

**Hawg-leg** (Hog-leg)**:** Large hand revolver of large caliber usually tied down outer leg.

**Heck-on-the- Hoof:** Uncaring and ornery while riding for the day.

**Heifer**: Full grown female (bovine) cow.

**Henry (lever) Rifle:** First brass and/or steel-framed lever rifle to combine the functions of ejecting fired case, self-cocking, self-loading, tube magazine fed, holding sixteen .44 caliber rimfire cartridges and done by the throw of the hand lever. *Mr. B. Tyler Henry* of the New Haven Arms Company received US Patent #30,446, on October 16, 1860. This famed rifle, of the Civil War and the frontier west, went into production in late 1860 and came to the market by 1862.

**Hombre:** (Spanish) Guy or fellow.

**Housewife:** Cowboy slang for a small sewing or mending kit with needles, snips, thread, sinew, buttons and like items.

**Howdy:** Contraction for; 'how-do-you-do', a basic western term of greeting.

**Improved Henry Rifle:** see Yellow Boy lever rifle.

**Indian flank side:** The right side of a horse in this context.

**Iron(s):** Slang for firearms in general, but mostly references to revolver or pistols.

**'John B':** Slang for the hatter, John B. Stetson, a Stetson or simply any cowboy hat.

**Lakota:** Also see Sioux

**Latigo string:** Braided leather lariat or lasso.

**Laudanum:** Opium based medicinal concoction used to abate chronic pain, addictive when used with frequency.

**Leather-pounders:** Horse riders with leather saddles.

**"Leavin' Cheyenne":** Term inferring departure or saying, 'good bye'. Loco: (Spanish) crazy or possessed with lunacy.

**Nefarious (Nefariously):** Evil, reprehensible, wicked, or immoral.

**Ne'er-do well-ers**: Never do well persons, or criminals

**O U T Spread**: The home ranch of Ornery and Slim, place named for its owner, *Mr. Oliver Ulysses Tucker*.

**Pard**: Short for 'Partner'.

**Pinto:** Spotted pony or horse, popular on the plains by cowmen and Indians.

Pistolero: (Spanish) Gunman.

**Pommel**: (noun) the knoblike bulge at the front and top of a saddlebow.

**Prairie coal:** Cow chips, dried cow manure patty.

Rancho (Spanish), for ranch.

**Recognisize** or **'ed** (ree-cog-ni-size): It's 'Ornery' for saying 'recognized.'

**Reckon'spect**: "Ornery and Slim" for 'reckon I expect.'

**Rememorate**: Ornery and Slim for, to remember or remembering.

**Reticule:** A small drawstring purse or lady's handbag.

**Riding rig:** A saddle.

**Roady:** Dusty, dirty or filthy items of clothing/baggage/persons from road/trail travel in these stories.

**'Roll**: (American Slang), short for payroll.

**Saddlers:** (America slang) for cowmen or cowboys.

**Sand**: Grit, courage or bravery

**Saw bones:** slang for doctor or surgeon.

Segundo (Spanish) for foreman, or supervisor of the ranch personnel.

**Sioux:** (In the context of Ornery and Slim, 1861 to 1900), A Native American tribe, speaking *Lakota*, one of the three major dialects, (Lakota/Nakota/Dakota) of the Sioux language. The most westerly tribe, the Lakota occupied; southeastern Montana, North and South Dakota, northeastern Wyoming and lower Saskatchewan, Canada. The seven branches of the Lakota are; Brule, Hunkpapa, Miniconjou, Oglala, Sans Arcs, Sihasapa, and San Arcs.
**Spendy:** (Slang) Costly or expensive.

**Stampede string:** A thin strapping devise of; braided, horse-hair or leather, single strip leather, usually attached to western style hats for keeping it on the head or neck of the wearer in wind or brisk riding.

**Straw Boss:** in this tale, foreman.

**Stingin' a whizzer**: The telling of tall tales or stories of fiction, usually humorous with a minor moral to the story.

**Teamster:** The driver of a team of burden animals, horses, oxen, cattle, etc.

**Tinker:** One who repairs or itinerant mender of house wares.

**Togs:** Clothing, duds, or outfits built for a specific craft or work.

**Tonie:** (Slang), highly fashionably, in vogue, in of great tone.

**Top Hand:** Highly experienced cowmen.

**Twenty Spread:** The neighboring ranch to the west-southwest of the O U T Spread, oft called the Double X or Dos X's by the vaqueros. The two X's representing the Roman numeral for 20.

**Un-disremember**: To recall or remember or recollect.

**Unnervey:** Cowboy speak for the loss of nerve or courage or spirit.

**Untried-pistol**: An unproven or "green" horse rider.

Vaquero/Vaquera: (Spanish) cowman/cowwoman (girl). (Vaquera, in this context is this author's creation, for it may not be found is Spanish-Mexican vernacular of this historical setting).

**Vittles** or victual; Food supplies, provisions, food for human consumption.

**Warbag:** A heavy canvas or burlap bag used like a suitcase by soldiers and cowboys.

**'whacked down**: Bushwhacked or shot dead.

**Wreck pan**: Dishpan

**WT**: Wyoming Territory; became a territory July 25, 1868 and the 44th state of the US on, July 10, 1890.

**Wyoming skirt:** Calotte style, ankle length appearing skirt, looking more like a dress than pants.

**XX Spread:** see the Twenty Spread.

**Yarn/yarns:** See Big windy

**"Yellow Boy" lever rifle**: The first model lever gun made exclusively by *Mr. Oliver Winchester's* (1810-1880), Winchester Repeating Arms Co, of New Haven, CT. Originally chambered to fire a .44 caliber rimfire metallic cartridge, this repeating rifle was known as the; Model 1866 Winchester/First Model Winchester/Improved "Henry" rifle and the "Yellow Boy" by the Plains Indians because of its brass rifle frame.

# About Your Author

Montana Kid Hammer, or 'Kid', is originally a Montana-native, an author and educator who lives just north of Fairbanks, Alaska. He enjoys horseback riding, snow skiing, hunting, reading history along side a good cup of "Arbuckles' Ariosa coffee" and cowboy action shooting. Kid has a family; six children, four grandchildren, is retired military, and has lived and traveled in the  region of which he writes. He is a recent graduate of the Institute of Children's Literature, is self-published locally about Alaska with an old west short-story volume, and has produced professional-technical submissions for the United States Air Force-Air Education and Training Command. He is also a NRA Certified Instructor and a Life-member of both the Single Action Shooting Society and the Golden Heart Shootist Society.

Printed in the United States
141956LV00002B/14/P